ALL IS FAIR IN LOVE AND DRUGS

CHAN

Published by Urban Chapters Publications.
http://www.urbanchapterspublications.com/

Acknowledgments

First and foremost I would like to thank god without him I wouldn't be here nor would I have the passion to write.

I would like to thank my mother Crystal through everything she has been there for me pushing me and encouraging me so for that ma I thank you and I love you more than words can express.

I would next like to thank my husband Mario for being the wonderful husband he is and supporting me through all the adventures I decided to choose I love you and thank you for being the wonderful husband and father you are (P.S. this book is set to release the day after your birthday so Happy Birthday my love :))

I would love to thank my big sister Kendra for being the best sister ever and encouraging me even when she didn't know she was encouraging me thank you.

I would like to thank my dear friend Queen Keishii without you love I would still be writing stories and throwing them away thinking they weren't good enough thank you for pushing me you're the best lets represent ;)

To my publisher Jahquel J thank you for believing in me love you're the best publisher in the world

Last but not least I would love to acknowledge my beautiful children Heaven, Ja'Niah & Ja'Ziah mommy loves you to the moon and back

It's to many people to thank name wise so all my friends who I texted late nights early mornings and for all my family and friends who supported me I love you and I can't thank you enough.

This book is in dedication to my grandmother Millie my grandfather Roby my brother Kendrick to my mother & father in law Mr & Mrs Fossett I love you all your gone but never forgotten

STASI

I was so pissed I allowed Marissa to talk me into coming out with her, because she never paid me any attention when we were out together. She was so caught up in her boyfriend Chris and the drinks he was buying her, that she never paid me any mind. *I don't give a fuck how many drinks they buy me, next time I'm staying my ass home*, I thought to myself. Just then, I heard my favorite song 'Tink Million' come on. *Ayeeee this my shit.*

"There's a million million reasons why I fuck with you," I sang along.

"Hey Stasi, that's your song ain't it!" yelled my best friend, Marissa. "Babe, I'm about to go hang with my girl. I don't want her thinking I dragged her out here to be in your face all night," Marissa told Chris.

"Alright baby, if you need me I'll be in VIP with the fellas," Chris stated.

Marissa walked over to her me, admiring how pretty I looked. Although I hated to admit it, I was a fine, dark-skinned sister. I stood at 5'3, had long, butt-length dreads, and was thick as hell–as I was always told. Marissa was light-skinned and was always looked at second when we were together. She was wearing a yellow Gucci bandage dress with some yellow Louboutin heels.

"So girl, are you happy you came out tonight? It's thicker than a bitch in here tonight," Marissa asked me.

"No hoe, I'm not happy I came. I'm so sick of you being all up Chris' ass, but you always inviting me somewhere. I don't want to be y'all fucking third wheel all the time; that shit is not cool."

"Girl, I swear you need some dick, because you always bitching; damn, loosen up a bit. If you stop being so stingy with the cat, maybe you'll have a man," Marissa laughed.

"You know what hoe, fuck you, I'm fine being celibate; less drama with a man and his hoes."

Just then, the DJ announced, "Listen up ladies, it looks like the big spenders are in the building tonight. Casey and his crew have entered the building."

The DJ then started playing Future's 'Fuck Up Some Commas,' and money started falling from the ceiling. See, what people didn't know was that the club was owned by the notorious drug king pin Javon, who people only knew as Jay. Casey was the right hand man of Javon, and silent partner of Club Capones, so anytime Casey stepped through Club Capones, he had to make it rain for the ladies.

"Girl, do you see these basic hoes throwing they selves all over the floor for that fucking money?" Marissa asked me as we looked through the glass floor of our VIP section.

"Girl, I see that and if I ain't have money of my own, my ass would be down there too, bitch; that's straight 100s falling from the ceiling, girl. They definitely got some cash. Them niggas always do that though girl, that's why it's so many bitches in here; you never know when Casey and his crew gon' fall through and make it rain."

CASEY

As I walked through the club to get to my private section that Javon had set up solely for me and our crew, females were pulling me left and right trying to be the one to get invited by me or someone in my crew to our VIP area. I stood at a good 6'6 at 26 years old. I was dark-skinned, but I wasn't what you call dark dark, if you catch my drift. I kept a low cut after cutting my dreads about 7 years ago. Me and my crew made it upstairs to our private section, and Javon already had me and the crew 30 bottles of Moët chilling on ice.

"Well my boys, it's been a long week, go ahead and find y'all some ladies to chill with and get on this moe; just make sure of your surroundings. You can never be too sure what is going to happen. Jack boys hate and broke hoe's scheme, so watch your intake on liquor tonight."

I came out with my crew occasionally, but never chose anyone to go to my section with me, so the ladies were coming at us hard.

"Here you go, Casey. Mr. Jay told me to go ahead and bring these over since this is the only thing you drink," the waitress Shanice advised me.

"Thanks shawty, here you go." I handed her a $100 tip.

"I can't take that, Mr. Jay said we aren't allowed to take any tips from anyone that sits in this section or from you," she said.

"Well shawty, let's just keep this a secret," I told her as I stuffed the hundred dollar bill in her bra.

"Thank you Casey; if you need anything, let me know," she said.

"No doubt shawty, I will. I'm going to make sure you leave here tonight with some decent money fucking with me and my crew. I know these broke ass niggas don't tip shit," I laughed as I shook my head.

"They damn sure don't, that's why I'm glad I'm head waitress, because I get to serve the VIP areas, but let me go before Mr. Jay cusses my ass out for being over here for so long," she said.

"Alright Shanice, I'll let you know when I'm ready for some more Patrón." Shanice walked off and went to the bar so she could serve her next VIP area.

I sat back sipping on my Patrón and checked out my surroundings, when my eyes happened to stop at the VIP area where two beautiful ladies were popping bottles and dancing like they had no cares in this cruel world.

"Damn, who is that chocolate sexy dread over there, baby fine as fuck. Marcus, come here real quick, let me ask you something bruh."

What up fam, who you looking at," Marcus said.

"Aye who those chicks over there," I said as I nodded my head towards the beautiful people.

"Oh, well the light-skinned chick with the long hair is that nigga Chris' girl, and that thick ass dark-skinned girl with the dreads is her best friend, Stasi; why, what's up man? You trying to get with one of them?"

"Nah man, I just wanted to know who the lovely ladies were; they been popping bottles left and right. I was just trying to see if they were with anyone."

"Yeah nigga, that's what your mouth say," Marcus said and walked off.

I decided to send the pretty ladies some bottles, hoping I would catch the attention of the pretty dread.

"Shanice, whenever you get a minute, let me holler at you."

"What's up Casey, what can I get for you?"

"I want you to take them some Patrón, Moët, Moscato, and Hennessy– and let the dread head know it's from me, alright?"

"Yes sir, I can definitely do that, I'll be back in a few. Do you want me to tell her anything else?"

"Nah, that's it. I don't want to scare her away or nothing like that, just handle that for me."

I swear, watching Shanice walk off and go get those bottles was pure torture for me. I couldn't help but pretend that I wasn't watching as she headed towards the VIP section with the drinks I requested for them. I watched as Shanice pointed to me, then shook her head, then headed out of the VIP booth.

"Fuck, I wonder what happened? Stasi doesn't look happy at all."

"Here you go, Casey; this is from Stasi. She told me to let you know you buying bottles doesn't do shit for her, and she's not a weak bitch that's impressed by bottles and bullshit hundred dollar bills falling from the ceiling when you walk in. She also said try a different approach next time you see her, or don't say anything at all."

My ego was a little hurt, but I definitely knew that me buying bottles for her wasn't going to win her over, so I was going to lay the charm on–and thick.

"Yo Casey, why that nigga Chris mugging you like a got a problem or some shit?" Marcus asked.

“Nigga probably mad cause I sent bottles to his bitch and her sexy ass friend, or he still thinking about when I beat his ass over Samantha’s slut ass last year.”

ONE YEAR AGO

I was feeling brand new as I walked out of Samantha's apartment, fixing my belt with the biggest grin on my face.

"Yo dude, why the fuck you coming out of my bitch house!" Chris yelled. I looked up at Chris like he had lost his damn mind.

"Are you really coming at me about this jump off bitch that everybody in the city has fucked?" I answered calmly. "Man, if you don't get the fuck out my face, I will beat you like you stole something from your mother."

"What the fuck you said about my mom, my nigga," Chris said as he pulled out his .9 millimeter.

I looked around and laughed.

"Dawg, put your gun down and fight me like a man; that gun ain't doing shit but pissing me off more."

I stood a good 6'6, and I towered over this punk by a good 3 inches or so. I had on a white polo shirt , True Religion jeans, and my wheat Timb boots. I always kept it simple, never flashy, with a small chain and my gold Rolex. I never wanted to make others feel like I forgot where I came from, and that was dirt poor.

Chris handed his gun to one of his workers and squared up; he looked around to see who was watching. I saw Chris check to make sure his bitch was watching, but I was about to embarrass his bitch ass for trying me. Before Chris could even collect his thoughts fully, I hit him with a punch so hard he flew back and knocked over two of his workers. I allowed Chris to get up, but as soon as he got up, I hit him two more times and left his ass knocked out cold.

"Tell that nigga when he wake up to fuck with somebody who won't beat his ass–next time I won't be so nice," I advised as I turned to leave.

Everyone that was watching just laughed at what they just saw and walked off. Samantha just shook her head and told her friend Valtenice to go get her some cold water. Samantha's friend brought her the water back, and she threw it on Chris' face. Chris hopped up and asked what happened.

"You just got your ass kicked out here acting a fool," Samantha advised

Ever since then, Chris has hated me, even though it was clearly his fault he got his ass whooped that day.

I looked up and noticed that Stasi was getting up and making her way towards the restroom; I knew this would be my only chance. Javon had set up restrooms specifically for the VIP people, just because they were very important people, and he felt like they shouldn't have to go to regular bathrooms with regular ass people. See, Javon had club Capones so decked out that people stood in line as early as eight pm on Saturday nights to ensure that they were in the club; that's just how live the club was. Club Capones was a two-story club; the VIP area had bulletproof glass all around, and was decked out with Versace couches, big screens, and it had its own bar areas and bathrooms. The lower level had three bars that were decked out, but with no furniture besides what was in the lower level VIP areas. The entire club was nice; that's why Club Capones was the 'go-to' spot. No one knew that the VIP area glass was actually bulletproof glass except Javon and I, because I helped build the club.

I made my way to the restroom areas and waited until I heard the water from the sink go off. I started walking past the women's restroom and boom–I ran into her literally.

"What the fuck, don't you watch where you're going, asshole!" Stasi yelled.

"I'm sorry beautiful, I wasn't paying attention, are you ok?" I asked with the smile that I knew drove ladies wild.

"Umm umm, yeah I'm ok," Stasi stuttered. I started laughing.

"Ok, well I just wanted to make sure I didn't knock that stutter into you." Stasi laughed and shook her head

“No you didn't, I just panicked for a second; you surprised me,” she informed me.

“Well, my name is Casey, beautiful lady, what is your name?” I couldn't beat around the bush anymore; I had to ask her.

“My name is Stasi, but I'm pretty sure you already know that by now,” she said.

“Possibly, but I just wanted to hear that accent of yours; where are you from?”

“I was born in Haiti but, I've been in Jacksonville all my life,” Stasi said.

“Oh so you’re Haitian? That's interesting,” I quipped with a smirk.

“I am, and why is that so interesting?” Stasi challenged.

“That explains why your skin is so beautiful and chocolate, and you have a hint of an accent,” I replied. Stasi busted out laughing.

“That was lame as hell, but cute,” she mentioned, “But let me get going before my friend starts looking for me,” Stasi said.

“Well, can I get your number, pretty lady?” I blurted out.

“Next time you see me, you can definitely have my number,” Stasi replied and walked off. *Damn she finer than a motherfucker,* I thought, *I'm definitely going to make her mine*. Stasi walked back to her VIP area with the biggest grin on her face.

STASI

What the fuck got into you that fast Marissa asked. “None of your business bitch let's wrap this up so I can go I got a case in the morning.”

Unbeknownst to everyone except for my best friend I was the highest paid lawyer with my own law firm. My father was also known as "*THE CONNECT*" which is why I was considered the baddest thing walking. My money and my daddy's money made me filthy rich.

Shanice came to clean up their VIP area and handed me back my black card.

"Was there anything else I could help you ladies with tonight?" Shanice questioned.

"No honey, you always do your thing when we come through, we have no complaints whatsoever," I told her. Shanice asked Stasi did she needed to know her total.

"Not really, but I know you are going to tell me anyway," I laughed.

"Of course I am, your total was $14,650."

"Ok love, it's on my card, and you know 20% is yours always, so that would be $ 2,930, but make it an even $3,000 so that my total is $17, 650," I advised. Shanice just stood there with her mouth wide open.

"Oh my God, are you serious? Stasi, like this is my biggest tip all night," Shanice said as she got teary-eyed.

"Yes I'm serious girl, you deserve it putting up with all this crap every night, and that's no offense to you; now go cash me out so I can get out of here girl, I promise you, it's no big deal." Shanice walked off quickly to go ahead and cash me out.

"I don't know why you be giving such big tips," Marissa grunted.

"I do it because I know she is doing something with her life; she's in school to be a nurse, and whatever I can do to help, I will. I can't take it with me when I die," I snapped as I rolled my eyes.

Shanice came back and handed me my receipt and thanked me about ten more times, gave me a hug, and walked off. I was beyond ready to go so I walked outside to the VIP valet and waited for them to pull my yellow G-wagon up. My car finally arrived, and I tipped the valet and hopped in and sped off.

CASEY

I was trying to figure out why Shanice was so excited over at Stasi's VIP area, so I decided to wait for her to come back to my VIP area so I could ask her.

"Ummm Shanice, what happened over there?" I questioned as she walked up.

"Man, I swear I love Stasi, she always hooks me up with the biggest tips, Casey; she just gave me a $3,000 tip." *Damn what the fuck does that chick do,* I thought. I didn't want to ask too many questions in one night and people get the wrong ideas and start throwing out rumors.

"Well go ahead and bring me my total, I'm ready to hit it," I warned her. Shanice walked off to get my total. She came back and I blurted out, "No, I don't want to know my total, yes I already know you're going to tell me what it is anyway," I said laughing. Shanice rolled her eyes.

“Look here, don't give me too much,” she said playfully. “Your total was $75,510, but Jay said don't worry about the 30 bottles of Moe if you don't want.” I rolled my eyes; I hated when this nigga tried to play me.

“Get the fuck out of here, I don't know why he trying to play me like that, take this and go ahead and give yourself a $5,500 tip shawty, my final total should be $81,010. Them young niggas paying for whatever else they brought though, that's not my job.” Shanice hugged me so damn tight that I thought I saw stars before she ran off to cash me out completely. I was happy that I could make her day and I knew with the money she made between me and Stasi she would be good for at least two or three months if she spent her money wisely. She gave me my final receipt and told me she would see me next week, like I'm always here.

“I'll see you next time shawty, keep your head up and keep doing big things,” I told her as I headed towards the back exit doors, so I could easily hop in my Lambo without being spotted.

JAVON

I was in my office going over all the money the club had made tonight. As me and Shanice went over everything, I was stunned to see that we had made over a million legal dollars tonight, not including the money that we had washed through the club. I sat back and smoked my blunt, ready for the day where I could finally say I was actually fully legit.

See, at first I only opened the club to wash my dirty money, but seeing the profit I had made in the four and a half months since it had been opened didn't hurt; I fell in love with Capones– it was my baby.

I was trying to figure out what was up with Shanice she was just staring at me. This girl has been trying to fuck me since day one but she wasn't anywhere near my type. I didn't want to fire her because she made me damn good money she was one fine woman but the way she stares at me scares me a little like she's in love or some shit. I was 5'9 and light-skinned, and people always tell me that I remind them of the rapper "The Game" minus the face tattoos. I looked up at Shanice and saw she was in a daze.

"Ayo ma, back to Earth," I snapped my fingers.

"I'm good Javon, is there anything else you need?" she asked

"Nah we good, thanks for working tonight," I said as I handed her five stacks. I don't know why but it seemed like Shanice wanted something more after I handed her her pay for tonight.

"You sure you good Shanice?" I asked

"Yes I'm sure well you know what I would like from never mind that's it I got to go." Shanice said then she ran out of my office.

I was happy that I was at the point where I was killing shit in the illegal business as well as in the legal business with my club. I thought back to seeing my homeboy Casey talking to Stasi and wondered if he knew exactly who she was. I laughed; he probably didn't know, but knowing my nigga, he was gon' do whatever he had to do to find out who she really was soon enough. I was happy to see she still hung with Marissa's fine ass after all these years. I didn't know why she was with that clown Chris. I couldn't do anything but shake my head and prepare to leave my office so the cleaning crew could do some work.

*

MARISSA

I was fresh out the tub, waiting on my man to come home and tend to my needs. I was horny as hell; we hadn't had sex in days. I was getting so sick of Chris acting like the streets was more important than me. What he failed to realize was even though I had been with him for two years, I just wasn't going to continue putting up with his bullshit.

'Ring, Ring'

"Yo, you reached Chris, you know what the fuck to do at the beep. One!"

I hung up. I wasn't about to leave his ass no fucking message–what the fuck did he think this was? I stood in the mirror and looked at myself. I was my worse critic. I was 5'3, light-skinned (mixed with Puerto Rican and black) and thick–not as thick as Stasi, but I was thick.

My hair was all mine and fell to the middle of my back. I felt like when I was with Stasi, guys stared at her or picked her first, because she was way more outspoken and I was somewhat shy.

"This nigga keeps playing, he gon' be by his fucking self and imma find me a real boss, somebody that actually wants to be with me!" I yelled out loud as I walked away from the mirror.

I went to my top drawer and pulled out a black La Pearle panty set, grabbed my robe, and decided to go ahead and lay down. After I put my robe on, I went ahead and put my hair in a messy bun, and looked at the clock; it was 4:30 am.

"See, this nigga got life all the way fucked up, I'm so done, I swear I am," I mumbled, completely fed up. I decided to go ahead and call it a night. I planned on spending all his money in the safe in the morning with my girl Stasi.

"Bitch better have my money" my phone went off

Ugh who the fuck is calling me, bitches can never let me sleep in, always aggravating me–damn. Where the hell did I put that stupid ass phone? Oh damn, there it is.

"What you want Stasi, I was sleep, damn–can you let a bitch sleep past 10 am?"

"Bitch it is past 10, it is fucking 1 in the afternoon, wake yo simple ass up," Stasi said. I hated when Stasi talked to me like I was beneath her not every body father sold drugs and shit this bitch was irking my nerves already.

“Girl I'm up, damn, and did you say one in the afternoon? Shit, I was sleeping good, that nigga ain't bring his ass home last night.”

“Yes I did say 1pm girl, please tell me why the fuck I see Chris walking around THE AVENUES MALL with some Spanish bitch and two kids?” Stasi asked.

“What the fuck did you just say?” I couldn't believe this shit.

“Girl you heard me, I done already took pictures and sent them to your iPad,” Stasi said. I scrambled out of the bed to find my Celine bag and iPad.

“I know this motherfucker is not trying me in fucking public!” I yelled; I was livid as fuck.

“No, you mean why the fuck is he trying you at all, Rissa! This shit ain't cool,” Stasi yelled.

I finally found my iPad mini 3 under all the junk inside my purse, and sure enough, as soon as soon as I opened it, there were ten pictures from Stasi, and three from an unknown number. I just shook my head; I couldn't believe him.

“This nigga got me so fucked up girl, like what the fuck is he thinking!” I yelled to my best friend.

“Girl hurry up, I'm down here waiting parked by the Buffalo Wild Wings; they just walked in to eat,” Stasi told me. I threw my iPhone 6 on the bed. I decided to throw on some True Religion shorts, an all-white tank top, and I slipped on my wheat Timbs.

I grabbed my iPhone, iPad, and my purse, then I locked up and left. I hopped in my pink Range Rover and sped the fifteen minutes to the Avenues Mall. I fumbled around in the hidden compact, making sure my

Tiffany blue .38 was still there. *Got it–oh yeah, these motherfuckers about to feel my wrath.* I swear, I barely parked before I was hopping out. I headed straight to my best friend. Stasi saw me approaching and knew I was ready to wreck some shit. She already knew not to say a word, and to just go along with me; that's just how we were when it came to certain situations.

"Where the fuck are they, Stasi? Show me right fucking now." Stasi just started walking towards Buffalo Wild Wings with me right behind her. Once inside BW3's, as they called Buffalo Wild Wings, we spotted Chris and the Spanish girl all hugged up. *This nigga got some fucking nerves*, I thought. I stood in front of Chris and the unknown chick for a good five minutes before one of the little girls that I couldn't even deny looked just like him spoke.

"Mommy, Daddy, somebody is standing right here looking at us." Both Stasi and I looked shocked, *Daddy?* Chris turned around, and as soon as he did, I punched the fuck out of him.

"What the fuck is this shit Chris? And why the fuck is she calling you Daddy?!" Chris just looked like he lost his best friend; he couldn't speak. The Spanish chick whose name was Lauren spoke.

"So I guess you are Marissa, and I guess Chris never told you about me or his twin girls," she said. Lauren could only shake her head and laugh; she didn't know why she put up with his shit for over 12 years. I looked from Lauren to Chris to the twins, and realized he'd been playing me the whole time; these kids looked to be around 5 or 6 years old. Chris just looked at me and pleaded.

"Just hear me out."

"Fuck you Chris," I said as I walked out of the restaurant. He had me so fucked up. I looked at Stasi and her ass was smiling but pretended to look sad. I knew her ass was happy I found out. What pissed me off the most was I really thought this bastard loved me and he had a whole entire family out here. I just wanted to get home and think this shit through before I really lost my mind. I was happy that I finally saw Chris for what he was and that was a low down, dirty dog.

CHRIS

Fuck I can't believe this shit just happened I thought to myself. Out of all the times I take my baby mama and kids out, Marissa just happens to see us. I had been with Lauren on and off for 12 years, and we had our daughters Carlee and Carleigh five years ago.

Lauren looked at me and said, "You don't wanna go after your wifey? We can wait, you know, you always make us wait when it comes to her anyway."

"Lauren, will you just shut the fuck up? Damn, I don't know why I even brought your fucking ass along!" I yelled. I had to get up and walk away from the table. I had to figure out how I was going to get my girl back; this shit wasn't supposed to happen. Being 5'11 and an ex-basketball player gave me a lot of chances to fuck all different types of chicks. Seemed like chicks went crazy over a light-skinned brother with a low-cut, six-pack, and a perfect smile. I was 32 and had hell of years' experience kicking games and a little bit of lies, so it took me nothing to get Marissa to fall into my trap of lies and deceit, but she was just so out of the loop that any brother that had cake and a big dick had a chance at her; it was probably wrong to say, but it took me nothing to hit that. Probably another reason why I only stayed with her so I could get down with Stasi and her people. I decided to go ahead and call Marissa's phone to see if she would answer.

"Hello, you reached Marissa Gonzalez. I'm sorry I can't get to the phone, please leave a message. If this is Chris' lying cheating ass, quit calling me bastard. Have a good day."

Man, I can't believe she put that on her voicemail. I decided to drive to Marissa's house off Baymeadows to this subdivision called Villa Medici, but I didn't see her pink Range Rover in the driveway. *Man, where the fuck this girl at, man?* I couldn't let the shit go down like this. I needed Marissa in my life; she was the only way for me to get plugged in with Stasi and the Haitian Cartel. My reasoning for keeping her around was truly selfish, but at that point I didn't give a fuck; I'd been trying for two years to get Marissa to talk to Stasi about me joining, but the bitch wasn't budging, and I was getting sick of her crybaby ass. All she had to do was shut the fuck up and put me in where I could make a shit load of money.

STASI

I sat and thought about my friend. I was really sad for her, but then again, I was so damn happy that she now had the time to meet someone who was really down for her. I swear, I always thought that Chris was nothing but a low down snake, and only using Marissa because he thought he could get in with me. I could never let that motherfucker do anything for me. I had no proof, but I'm sure I would have it soon enough and be able to prove that he was only using Marissa to get him into the Haitian Cartel.

Let me introduce myself. My name is Stasi Boudreaux, and I'm 26 years old. I'm what you would call the connect's daughter, and I could put anybody on before I finished tying my shoes, if I wanted to. However, if I felt like you weren't going to profit me or my father any money, or if I felt like you were a big snake, then there was no point in me wasting my time. I had been feeling like some things were off with Chris, but could never pinpoint what it was.

Marissa was my best friend, and had been since we were nine years old. I used to visit all the time before my dad let me actually move here when I turned fourteen. Marissa didn't have a lot, so she always got picked on and me being the person I am, I gave her whatever I didn’t want. I knew that Rissa wanted Chris put on so bad so she could shine like me, but I felt that if I had to grind and get it, so did the next motherfucker. I wasn’t into always giving handouts; it defeated the purpose of me working my ass off while she sat at home and did nothing. Marissa was my best friend but she didn’t seem to care if she had a job and how her bills were paid. She always expected the next motherfucker to do it for her and that was what pissed me off, I swear if she got off her ass and made an effort shit would be so much better for her. I remembered that I hadn't talked to my dad in over a week and that was weird because we normally texted, emailed, or Face-Timed at least three times a week I hoped everything was ok.

TWELVE YEARS AGO

"mwen Dont vle papa," (i don't want to papa) yelled a 14 year old me.

"pitit fi ou dwe aprann sa a," (daughter you must learn this) said her father Janeiro.

My dad wanted me to be the biggest Queen Pin in the world before I hit twenty-seven. See since my dad was born and raised in Haiti, growing up being the most outspoken everyone followed him so it was nothing for him to have people who listened to everything he said. My dad had the best of the best coke you could step on it 8-10 times and the fiends would still be on cloud 10. He told me he had always wanted a boy but for some reason God only blessed him with me. My mom passed away while she was giving birth to my brother, Stacey but they both didn't make it. I know it hurt him to have his wife and only son die and there was nothing he could do to bring them back. So my dad was all I had and vice-versa he vowed that before he took his last breath that I was going to be filthy rich an working for myself with motherfuckers working for me.

"papa mwen vle yo jwe" (dad I want to play) I sighed although I wanted to be a queen pin and be the female version of my dad, but I didn't want to do it at 14 years old.

"ban m 'yon pitit minit" (give me a minute child) my dad said. I rolled my eyes; I knew all I had to do was ask one more time and I would be on my way to play with my friends.

"ale pi devan lanmou mwen" (go ahead my love) my dad said, he just couldn't deny me what I wanted even if he wanted to. He laughed she had him wrapped around his finger.

THE PRESENT
STASI

I decided to go ahead and call my father to see what was going on with him.

"*Ring, Ring*"

"sak pase? ki novel?" (how are you what's new?) My father asked upon answering.

"anyen dutou papa m'songe'w" (nothing new papa I missed you) I replied.

I missed my dad so much. I wished that he would come live in the states, but he told me that he could never return because he was a wanted man. I knew one of the main reasons was he wanted to make sure nobody messed with his coke, so he could reprimand them himself instead of having someone do it for him. That's just how my dad was.

“When are you coming to visit, my child?" He asked. I don't know why my dad asked me this question every time I spoke with him, knowing that I absolutely hated going to Haiti. Knowing my father he just wanted to see me to make sure that everything was okay and I was in perfect shape.

"im pa vini papa mwen rayi kote sa a (I'm not coming papa I hate that place). My father knew that I wouldn't just come to Haiti just to visit no matter how much he begged. The only reason I went to Haiti was to lead the monthly meetings.

"Well my child I was so busy making sure everything was in order for you that I didn't have a chance to call please forgive me"

Janeiro stated. I was happy now that I knew my father was working and not tricking off on the young tricks in Haiti.

I knew that he never brought any women around me, since my mother Talia passed away. I wondered how he managed? He was a very handsome man. My dad was 59 but didn't look a day over thirty. He was 6'5, had this lovely sun-kissed butter pecan skin with a beard that you had to get close to in order to notice the grey in it. Marissa used to be in love with my dad back in the day; it was ridiculous.

"Well I gotta run, my child; I promise to FaceTime tomorrow so we can have a longer conversation mwen renmen ou," (love you) Janeiro stated.

"mwen renmen ou too papa," I replied as I hung up.

I decided that I wanted to spend some money just for the hell of it, but there were absolutely no places to shop in Jacksonville where I could spend my money. I decided that I would treat Rissa to a shopping trip to get her mind off that butthole of an ex Chris, but I definitely would remind her that this wasn't something she should get used to.

I went ahead and called Marissa to see if she wanted to make the 2-hour trip to Orlando with me, then possibly Miami depending on how we felt after we tore down the mall in Orlando. I just pray she wasn't doing all that whining, cause lawd I couldn't take it.

MARISSA

"Bitch better have my money" my phone went off. *I know this ain't nobody but Stasi's ass calling to bother me like always*, I shook my head.

"What the lick read youngin," I said as I answered the phone and finished drying off.

"Girl I'm trying to see what you got going on round there, are you ready to ride to the O so we can blow up some commas?" Stasi started singing.

"Girl keep your day job, 'cause singing is not one but yes girl, you know I don't mind spending money that isn't mine," I quipped.

Stasi yelled, "Well you got 45 minutes or you getting left, young hoe" then she hung up. *I hope this hoe don't think that I want her to spend her money on me, cause my nigga was caught cheating or whatever the hell he was doing.* I thought to myself.

I walked to the closet and looked around. I was kind of happy that I had just got out the shower, or Stasi would really be leaving my ass. I decided to keep it simple but cute, so I grabbed some form fitting True Religion shorts that made my ass look wonderful, a tan V-neck True Religion shirt that made my breasts sit up and say hello at first glance, and my favorite tan UGGs. I really didn't care whether it was hot or cold, I wore these damn UGGs rain, sleet, or snow, because they were so comfortable to walk in for hours at a time, especially shopping with Stasi's ass. I decided to set it off with my all-gold Cartier watch, and my favorite 14-carat Tiffany earrings. I threw my hair in a messy bun with a tiny touch of lip gloss. I really hated any kind of make-up, but I loved a little shine to my full lips.

I went to the safe that Chris keep under my California King bed and took 20g's out of the 90 g's that Chris left in the safe, and dropped it into my tan Celine bag. Just as I was about to text Stasi and ask her where her ass was, I heard a horn and loud music. I ran downstairs and headed to the front door to go ahead and lock up so we could ride out. I walked outside and pulled my Tom Ford shades down.

"Damn it's hot as fuck out here," I sighed.

"Hey bihhh, i missed you, I ain't seen you in a few days," Stasi said.

"Girl why the fuck was you in my window watching me get dressed," I joked. I looked at Stasi and shook my head. I swear, we thought so much alike that it was funny. I guess that's what being friends damn near your whole life did to you; you started thinking and acting alike. Stasi had on a white V-neck True Religion shirt that made me take a second glance; her breasts were fucking huge. She wore some black form-fitting True Religion shorts, and her glittery black UGG boots. She topped it off with a black Cartier watch and 16-carat diamond studs, with a small chain that made you have to wear shades just to look at it. My girl always came out ready to shit on a bitch's life, and she didn't even try; it just happened, especially the way she carried herself.

"I can't believe we are wearing identical outfits girl we think so much alike." I said

I know Stasi was ready to hit the road; she had already gassed up, so she turned on her satellite radio and we tuned into Mytenacity radio, with our favorite DJ Swagg the crowd pleaser. He had us so turned up that the usual 2-hour drive ended up being 1 hour and 15 mins. We found a parking spot at The Florida Mall and started walking towards the entrance, ready to hit up our favorite stores.

CASEY

“Mannnnn who those chicks is right there, Von,” I said to my right hand and best friend Javon. Javon looked over his shades

"Bruh, I think that's Stasi and her girl Marissa. I know them asses from anywhere, B,” Von started laughing.

"Ayo, we gotta catch up to them man, I'm tryna holla at Stasi forreal,” I said as I rubbed my hands together. I couldn’t help but fantasize about my head between her thick, chocolate thighs; just thinking about it was making my dick hard as fuck. Von laughed, but I knew he knew I was serious about what I said.

"Man, I'm just happy Marissa ain’t with that square Chris no more; remember when you beat him up in the hood about that shit with that hoe Samantha?” We both laughed.

We decided to speed up a little bit so it looked like we ran into them randomly and not like we were following them, even though we kind of were. Stasi and Marissa were headed into Victoria’s Secret for the semi-annual sale.

"Girl you ain’t gon’ believe that Chris told me to keep all the money that was in the safe at my house. I mean, I wasn’t going to give it back to his ass anyway, but still."

"Well hoe, did you bring some money instead of trying to spend all mine?" Stasi laughed.

"Shut up heffa, I did dang, let's quit talking and get all we can before the ratchets come in here trying to get all the good stuff," Marissa said. After 45 minutes, the women left, spending over $300 apiece, but they had everything they needed from bras to panties, lingerie, hoodies, sweats, and duffle bags. As they walked out the store, I said, “It's about time we ran into each other again. I thought you were hiding from me.” Stasi and Marissa turned around, and lo and behold, me and Javon were standing there with the biggest smiles on our faces.

Damn, shorty so bad, I wonder what she got in them bags; I bet it's something that her ass is just going to swallow, I thought to myself.

"Well, whenever you done mind fucking me Casey, you can look at my face, ok?” Stasi joked. Marissa and Javon busted out laughing like they were in high school.

"My bad shorty, my mind was just roaming, how have you been beautiful?" I asked.

“I've been well, thank you for asking,” Stasi answered. I could tell by the way shawty was staring at me that she was definitely feeling me. I loved that she wanted to play hard to get because, I always got what I wanted. When you’re done mind fucking me beautiful, I’d love for you to let me walk and talk with you.” Marissa and Javon had already gone and kicked it off and left us to get better acquainted, which was definitely a good thing.

JAVON

Man, I swear I felt like a kid in the candy store. I'd been trying to get at Marissa since I first seen her in Pure and her friend told me she was taken. *I've just been waiting on that nigga to slip so I can treat her like a real man is supposed to*, I thought to myself. Another man's trash is another man's treasure.

"So Javon, what's been going on? I haven't heard anything from you in about two years. I mean, I see you here and there, but you never speak," Marissa questioned me.

"I've just been waiting in the cut until it was my time baby, that's all," I said jokingly, although I wasn't joking. I didn't know why she had been giving me a hard time. I was hard working and sexy as hell, so I've been told; and loyal. I heard she wasn't big on the player type of guys, which I definitely wasn't. Yeah I fucked hoes, but they already knew I wasn't for the shit and I didn't have a main woman for them to compete with unless Marissa gave me a chance. "So why have you been running from me for so long? It's been a few years," I argued.

"I haven't been running from you, I'm just aware of who I spend my time with, and you my dear man are one of the biggest players this world has seen," she said.

"Now see, that is where you are all wrong. I treat my woman right and make her feel like the queen she is; I don't creep, nor cheat. If I have to do that, then there is no reason for us to still be together," I protested." Marissa just sat and looked at me for a second.

"Well, that is to be determined, Mr. Burns," she said to me.

"Oh, we are on last name status now, huh, Ms Gonzalez?" We both laughed." Come on ma, let's finish shopping; we been playing and my black card burning a hole in my pocket," I said as I grabbed her hand and started walking through the mall to go ahead and swipe my life away.

Me and Marissa spent the next three hours going from True Religion to the Polo Factory, to Dillard's, Footlocker, BCBG, Michael Kors, Tom Ford, and Louboutin. We spent over $80,000, and I really didn't care because I knew sooner than later, Marissa was going to be my lady, and this would be a regular activity for the both of us. I turned to Marissa.

"Yo baby, go ahead and call your home girl and let her know we about to head back to the Ville, and ask her if it's cool if my man Cas rides back with her." Marissa quickly pulled out her iPhone and called Stasi.

"Hey sis, Javon wanted to know if it was ok if Casey rode back with you? We about to head back home," Marissa said.

"Girl, you just gon' up and leave me like that? But nah, y'all can go ahead, we were thinking about going to Universal Studios in a minute anyway, so bye bitch, be safe," Stasi joked.

STASI

I hope my girl takes her time; I don't want her getting hurt anymore, but then again, Javon ain't like that I thought to myself.

"So Casey, are you going to be scared on these rides, 'cause I don't got time for that," I asked.

"Girl, if you don't hush and come on, we taking your truck or mine? You know I have a condo here too, so we can drop your truck off or leave mine there, it doesn't matter," Casey told me.

"Well, we can go ahead and drop my truck off. I don't feel like driving anyways."

"Follow me then beautiful, my condo is about 10 minutes away, so it's not that far."

I followed behind Casey and his all black Porsche Cayenne SVU, and thought, *damn I need to get me one of these and customize that bitch out.* I had over twenty vehicles ranging from Porsches to Benz's to g-wagons; some people called it excessive, but I called it options. People could never know when or what car I would be riding through the city in, because I never drove the same car twice in a week, much less the same month. I also just loved being able to purchase anything I wanted whenever I wanted; money was never a option to me, and had never been since I was growing up. We finally arrived to Casey's condo, and I was actually impressed; it was a nice high-rise condo on the 26th floor of The Carling. We walked into the condo, and I was utterly impressed; his condo was all black and decked out with powerful figures such as President Obama, Martin Luther King Jr., Malcolm X, Rosa Parks, and

Michelle Obama. I was in love; not only did he have such powerful pictures, but his furniture was nice as well.

"Would you like a tour, baby?" Casey asked me.

"No, I'm good. I don't want us to get caught up talking politics; just looking around I'm impressed, and I'm not easily impressed."

"Well thanks baby that means a lot. I tried, and I decorated myself," he said with a big smile.

"Where's your bathroom? I want to change before we go to the theme park."

"Down the hall to the left; don't stink my bathroom up either, girl," Casey yelled behind me.

I can't believe I'm really chilling with this man, I thought to myself. This was so unlike me but it was something I needed and honestly wanted if it was the right time and person.

CASEY

"Girl, it's been about three weeks since you came to see me." Trey Songz played in the background.

I sipped on my Patrón and thought about all the things I've been wanting to do to Stasi. I couldn't help but wonder the mystery behind her? Did her parents die and she inherited a shit load of money? Did she date a drug dealer and he kept her laced with money? I hoped it wasn't the lather, because I definitely wanted her to myself. I had to know her story and not the one she just told people, so they didn't continue to ask questions. I didn't want to pacified a lie. I wanted the hardcore truth so I could decide whether I wanted to fuck with her exclusively or not. I knew that yellow G-wagon set her back a good $120K probably more because she had it customized. I was definitely a car's man and I knew that one was one hell of a car.

Damn, I wonder what's taking her so long, I thought.

STASI

Damn now I don't even feel like going anywhere no more, I thought as I stepped out the shower. *I know this man probably thinking what the fuck am I doing but I had to get fresh; I was hot and sweaty,* I thought, disgusted as hell.

"Yo Stasi, you good?" He said, as he knocked on the bathroom door.

"Yes Casey I'm good, I just decided to hop in the shower before I changed, hope you don't mind," I yelled, through the door.

"Ok baby, I already showered and changed. I'm ready to go; hurry yo fine ass up," He yelled back.

"He just doesn't know what I really want to do to his ass, goodness," I uttered. I decided to keep it simple, so I chose to wear an all-yellow pink tracksuit and my all white Jordan 1's. I finally walked out of the bathroom to join Casey.

"Ta-daaaaa," I said, as I spun around so he could see me.

"You look damn good ma, that outfit doing something to me; hope I don't have to knock nobody out while we out there now," He said. He cut off all the lights and followed me to the door, not able to take his eyes off me.

CASEY

I can't believe I'm finally chilling with her, I thought as we headed towards Universal Studios.

"I love your truck, Casey. I swear, I'm thinking about getting me one of these and customizing it," Stasi told me. She looked around the truck and I could tell she was absolutely in love; the truck had nice leather seats, three rows, and a touch screen in the front, and it ran wonderfully.

"Alright ma, we here, let's have some fun," I said as I walked around to let her out. We decided to get on the Incredible Hulk first, and I almost had a heart attack but I wasn't going to let her know that I couldn't allow her to make fun of me.

"Are you ok baby, you seem a little scared," Stasi asked me playfully.

"Girl hush, I'm good, I just choked a little bit," I laughed with her. Truth was, I almost shit my pants, but I damn sure wasn't about to say anything she took that ride like a G and I bitched up. We explored everything, from the Harry Potter section to the Jurassic Park ride, and even some of the not so scary rides, like the Simpsons ride. We were having so much fun we didn't even realize we had been there for four hours and hadn't eaten anything yet.

We decided to grab something light to eat before heading back to my condo. We decided on burgers and fries, something light but enough to get us full.

"Damn, I don't know if this shit is good or if I'm just hungry. I ain't ate all day," Stasi said.

"Me either ma, running around all day with Javon and then you, I just lost track of time. I don't want to sound nosey, but what's your story, ma? What's there to know about Stasi Boudreaux?" I asked as I drunk my tea.

"Well, my name is Stasi Boudreaux, and I am the number one attorney in Jacksonville and all surrounding areas. My law firm is Boudreaux and Associates. I graduated from Clark Atlanta University. I was born in Haiti 26 years ago, and I was back and forth between Jacksonville and Haiti until I turned 14 and my dad allowed me to move here with my aunt. I've known Marissa since she was 10 and I was 9; we've been damn near sisters ever since then. I haven't had a boyfriend the past six years, just because I couldn't trust anybody to be with me for me and not my money," Stasi said.

"I guess I should start now," I said, "Well I'm 26, I've known Javon since I was 13; we've both been on the streets grinding trying to make life better for ourselves. For the past 7 months, he's been set on going legit, and I'm just focusing on making sure my future wife and my kids and their kids and their kids are set for life," I told her honestly. I didn't know if we were going to be together, but I wanted her to know that I wasn't leaving the drug game anytime soon. "I'm also a silent partner at Club Capones. My parents were never in my life; my grandma raised me and honestly, without her, I don't know where the fuck I would be at right now. I'm also Haitian, though I've never set foot in Haiti. For some reason, my grandma hates that place, but she won't tell me why."

"Well, I'm glad we met and I hope that we bring some sunshine to each other lives," Stasi said. I couldn't help but sit back and think about what she told me. I knew she pacified me because, just being a lawyer didn't or couldn't have her with that much money. I was going to be cool about it though and wait until she decided to tell me what her REAL story was, because her just being a lawyer wasn't the only thing that she did.

MARISSA

“I wonder if those two love birds are enjoying themselves at the theme park.”

“Ain't no telling with them two crazy asses; you know Casey is Haitian too, right?” Javon asked.

“You got to be kidding, Stasi's ass is Haitian, but she doesn't tell anybody, I mean anybody; I don't know why. You can hear her accent when she gets pissed off, or if you hear her speaking creole to her dad.”

“Enough about them though, baby. I just want to let you know I'm really happy you at least chilled with me for today; it's been a long time coming. I knew I wanted you from the first time I saw you in PURE two years ago. I was just waiting until you realized you wanted me too,” he told me sincerely.

“Honestly Javon, I been through so much shit in my 27 years that I could never tell who was sincere and who wasn't. But honestly, just being with you the last twelve hours, you definitely are sincere and I'm happy for that.”

“What did you want to eat, Rissa?” he asked me.

“Honestly, I don’t care Javon, long as we are still chilling I'm good.” We decided to go to Chili’s and keep it simple and sweet, and continue to get to know each other.

“Welcome to Chili’s, my name is Tiffany, I'll be your waitress tonight. Come with me and I'll show you to your booth,” the waitress said as she led us to our booth. “I'll be with you shortly,” she told us as she seated us and walked off.

"So tell me about yourself, Javon. I barely know anything about you, yet I'm so comfortable with you."

"Well I'm 26, and I'm the only child; my mother passed when I was 15, which is what led me to the streets, and my father? Well, let's just say fuck him, because he was never there for me, even after he found out my mother passed. He came to see if she left him any money, and when I told him no, he left again and I haven't seen the bastard since. I'm the owner at Club Capones, you know, the club that you frequent so often/ I also have a master's degree in business, and I am honestly trying to get out of the game," he admitted.

"Well, I guess I can speak about myself," I whispered.

"Can I take your drink orders?" the waitress interrupted.

"I'll take the 2-4-1 Hennessy and Coke. And she'll take a Strawberry Patrón margarita," Javon ordered for us.

"As I said before, I'm 27, I'm Puerto Rican and Black, and I'm the only child as well. My mom raised me; my sperm donor basically decided that I wasn't his child, but comes in my life ever so often wanting to claim me, then the next minute he doesn't. It gets to the point where I'm like fuck him, I don't need him, because he breaks my heart every time. Once I stop wishing and hoping my dad is in my life, he just reappears and then leaves, and hurts me again," I cried. "I guess that's why I couldn't give a fuck about him. All my life I dated wanna be drug dealers, or supposed to be plugs. I'm just trying to get my life where I want it, where I don't have to feel like I'm searching for love or a father figure, but where I actually have a man that cares for me mentally, physically, and emotionally."

"Here's your drinks, are you all ready to order?"

“Yes, we both would like the house salads with ranch; she doesn't want any tomatoes or cucumbers, and add extra ranch–that's all,” Javon said as he handed her the menus. I just sat and looked at him, trying to figure out how the hell he knew what I liked to eat without me having to tell him.

“I know you’re wondering how I know that. Let's just say your best friend helped me do my homework,” he laughed. We sat and continued to get to know each other; we didn't even realize how much time had passed. We had been talking and drinking for well over three hours, until Casey called Javon.

“Aye bruh I got you on speakerphone, so watch your mouth, B.” Javon answered.

“Bruh, what the hell y’all got going on? Y’all made it back safely?” Casey asked.

“Yeah, we made it back a couple of hours ago; we been sitting in Chili’s kicking it. We ain't even realize we been here for three hours, bruh,” Javon explained.

“Damn, y’all been kicking it really good, huh man?” Casey laughed.

“Man shut ‘yo egg head ass up, what you want man, I'm tryna kick it with my girl,” Javon joked.

“I ain't want nothing man, just wanted to kick it with you and to make sure y’all was good. Me and Stasi headed back to the crib. Our asses were at Universal Studios earlier, and we had a fucking blast man. But look, I'm going to go ahead and get off this line, so I can keep my eyes on the road, I'll hit you tomorrow so we can handle business, be easy bruh, love ya,” Casey said.

“Love you too my boy, holla at me tomorrow,” Javon said as he hung up.

“You two are really like brothers huh?” I asked

“Yeah that’s my brother. I love him to death and just as if we had the same mother and father” Javon answered.

CHRIS

Man, I can't believe Marissa is in here with this nigga Javon. I mean, I don't got beef with dude, but he hang with that bum, Casey. So I definitely can't allow him to be with my girl, I thought to myself. I was seated in the far corner of Chili's with my on again off again jump off and baby mama, Samantha. I always kept her hidden, because I didn't want anyone clowning me for knocking a known hoe up, and also for times when Marissa was mad at me and decided she wanted to be on her bullshit. I wanted to make sure I had somewhere to go, plus the bitch sucked a mean dick–I don't think I could ever deny that.

"So Chris, are you going to pay attention to me, or that bitch Marissa and her fucking date all night?" Samantha said. "I'm so sick of you treating me like shit. I do everything that you like. I suck, fuck cook and clean. I take care of our son and it's only a limited amount of people that even knows he exists. I'm so over this shit, I've been running behind you since middle school and you still can't act right" Samantha yelled.

I never paid her any mind back then because she was skinny as hell and had bad acne. Now she was a solid 5'5 thick as fuck in all the right places. Her skin was smooth as a baby's ass and she was a big time freak. Plus, she was loyal than a motherfucker; I couldn't deny that. I just couldn't see her like that, because she still lived in the hood. I couldn't have my woman dead center in the middle of the hood; that was easy access to all the stick-up kids, and I wasn't with that.

After watching them for another five minutes, I finally decided enough was enough, and got up and walked to the table where Javon and Marissa were sitting at waiting on their check.

"So Marissa, I see you hanging with scums now," I sneered. Javon looked at me with the look of death.

"No Chris, I don't hang with scums. I hang with REAL MEN that have my best interest at heart–you know, something you didn't have with me," she sneered. I watched Javon sit back and smirk like it was some kind of show to him. I wanted to knock his ass out, but I decided to give him a pass for now. I wanted to know why he was here and with my bitch at that.

"What the fuck did you just say to me bitch!" I growled as I moved towards Marissa. Javon jumped up calmly and looked at me. I almost ran but I wouldn't give him the satisfaction of seeing me a tad bit scared. This nigga wasn't God.

"Yo, if you don't back the fuck up off my girl, I'm going to handle you the way my man Casey did last year over your BABY MAMA,Samantha over there," He said, as he nodded towards Samantha.

Marissa looked towards the table, and sure enough, Samantha and our son sat together watching. I watched Marissa carefully, knowing that she would blow up at the drop of a hat. It surprised me that all she did was shake her head and turn back towards the table as if nothing happened. I watched her as she went in her bag pulled out $100, which was more than enough to cover the bill and grabbed Javon's hand and exited the restaurant. I swear, I was livid, and now I had to kill both of them for embarrassing me in front of the entire restaurant. I figured maybe I was going to fuck Marissa in front of Javon and then kill them both, but not before I was put on or took over the whole fucking organization.

JANEIRO

"Tout bagay anfom? (Is everything ok?) Kisa? (What) Ki moun? (Who?) Kile? (When?)" I asked my spy.

"mwen pa konnen (I don't know)"my spy stated.

"byen chèche konnen!" (well find out) I yelled as I hung up the phone. I don't know why he acts like he knows nothing at all. I was trying to find out who this kid was that my daughter was hanging with, and if he could be beneficial to us; it takes a lot to be with our organization. I know my daughter did her homework; she never let anyone in without knowing everything there was to know about them. That aspect she learned from me; any time anyone came around, I did a background check on them, and then asked them to see if they would answer with what I had discovered. If not, their entire family died in front of their eyes, and then I killed them. That had kept me off the FBI's radar for years and years; I think it was the best decision I came up with. As I sat on the balcony, I rubbed my beard and thought about the day that I lost my son and my wife while she was giving birth to my son.

21 YEARS AGO

Mwen renmen w (I love you) wè ou talè (see you soon)," my wife Talia cried as she was wheeled to the operating room to have an emergency C-section.

Mwen renmen my love, see you soon!" I shouted as my wife was wheeled away.

"Papa, where is Mommy going?" Stasi questioned me.

"She is about to go have your baby brother; they will be out soon; we just have to wait a while." I had the entire labor and delivery floor blocked off; no one was allowed in or out. I had my security covering the entire hospital so no one would bring harm to my family.

I was a little skeptical because I had heard that my rival "Black" wife worked at the hospital that my wife was about to deliver my son at. However, I've done extensive background checks on everyone and when I say everyone that's a understatement. I did background checks on the CEO of the hospital all the way down to the people that emptied the garbage, and thankfully nothing came up otherwise we would've had a big problem.

"Family of Talia Boudreaux," the head doctor said.

"Right here we're right here," I bragged with the hugest grin on my face.

"I'm very sorry to tell you this sir; your wife nor your son made it."

"What the fuck did you say to me?" I growled as I grabbed the doctor's scrubs. "You come out here and tell me my fucking wife and son

are dead? You simple motherfuckers couldn't deliver a fucking baby!" I snapped.

"SIR SIR, there were complications; she just stopped breathing," the doctor mumbled.

"I want the names of every fucking person that walked into that fucking operating room with my wife and kid, or you're fucking dead, do you understand me?" I yelled to the doctor.

"Yes sir, I'm on it right away," the doctor stuttered as he ran away. I didn't know what the fuck was going on, but these motherfuckers had picked the wrong one to try and play with, cause I will burn this bitch down with everyone and their family inside if they couldn't give me a good explanation of what happened.

*

THE PRESENT (JANEIRO)

As I sat reminiscing, I still couldn't believe my wife and son were gone. They were my everything; now my everything was Stasi, and making sure she ruled the world. Right now, our empire was worth $500 billion and growing. I was the connect's connect, and everybody came to me for the purest cocaine. I also had the best pills, weed–shit, anything you needed, I had. I only showed my face to certain people, and there was a system to be invited in. You didn't just get asked; you had to have a certain way that you carried yourself.

If you have ever heard of the Cartel, then just think of me as the leader and ruler of the Haitian Cartel, which consisted of five families.

They were supplying everyone from the US, Paris, Canada, and Asia to Europe–you name it, I supplied it, and I was well respected. I made sure everyone knew of my daughter and my expectations of her when I was gone, and if they didn't like it, they would pay with death. There was absolutely NO DISRESPECT TOLERATED. If you felt someone from the families or the people they were supplying could potentially be harmful to the Haitian Cartel, then you would request a meeting and announce what you had with supporting documents, or else you and your entire family were killed for false accusations.

I had been running the Haitian Cartel very well for over 25 years, and I felt that I had another 25 in me; even at my age of 59, people told me I didn't look a day over 30. The only way you would know my age was my beard. I exercised and ate healthy and all. The young women here loved to try to get close to me; a lot of them said I looked like a light-skinned Morris Chestnut–go figure. I never let anyone close to me though, just because you can never tell a person's motives. I wanted to be on earth to see my daughter get married and have kids and then to see her kids have kids. My favorite line was "Bosses move in silence" and I damn sure didn't talk a lot. I was straight forward and to the point. If you couldn't handle that then too bad so sad.

STASI

I felt as if someone was watching us all of a sudden. I had this eerie feeling come over me and that only happened when something was wrong.

"Um Casey, I think we should head back to your place, something isn't right."

"Ma we good, we're at a theme park, what's the worst that could happen?" he questioned me.

"Let me explain this very quick; you don't know who the fuck I am and what I'm capable of, but I promise you're going to learn, and very quick–somebody is watching us, so let's fucking go!" I shouted.

"Alright ma damn, we can go, but I thought you just told me who you were," Casey admitted, now confused.

"I told you some things about me, not all; you're not ready for everything right now," I replied angrily. We were headed through a crowd of patrons when someone grabbed my hand and tried to pull me away from Casey. I tried not to scream, but the shit caught me completely off guard.

"Casey, I don't know what the fuck is going on, but someone has my hand and they're trying to pull me, help me," I expressed to him. I wasn't scared, because I knew this came with the territory but damn, in the middle of a theme park? Whoever this was, they were bold as fuck– shit is just crazy man. Casey was finally able to get me free, and we walked out of the park and headed towards his Cayenne, and peeled out of the parking garage.

"Now tell me exactly WHO the fuck you are," he demanded.

“I’m Stasi Boudreaux, and I am THE CONNECT and second leader to the Haitian Cartel. There's some things that I don't think you are ready to know, nor am I ready to tell you yet,” I replied. He started laughing.

“Yeah right, the leaders of the Haitian Cartel are all men,” he stated. All I could do was shake my head and laugh.

“Haha, that's what we wanted everyone to think; it’s not my time to completely take over, so there’s no reason to reveal who I am. It is only for the families under the Cartel to know.” In the middle of our conversation, my phone went off.

BZZZZZ.ZZZZZZ.

Papa: nou bezwen pale (we need to talk)

ME: sou sa Papa (about what dad)

Papa: parèy la ou se amizan m ' pitit (the fellow you are entertaining me child)

ME: te ke ou nan pak la (was that you at the park)

My father never replied back. Mwen (my) papa (dad) se (is) fou (crazy), I chuckled more so to myself than anyone else.

“Kisa (what) rive (happened) bèl (beautiful)?” Casey asked.

“My papa just texted me asking about you. I don't know why I wasn't thinking before we went anywhere that his ass knows every fucking thing,” I sighed.

“Are we going to have a problem, Stasi? I really like you, but I don't want any beef between you and your father. I know he is all you have,” Casey expressed.

“We’re good my love, now let's hurry and make it to your house. I'm tired and ready to relax.” I sat back and tried to relax, although this damn man was doing damn 100 mph all the way back to his condo. I didn’t know what to do. I wasn’t mad that my father found out about Casey, but I didn’t know if I really wanted Casey to know exactly who I was.

MARISSA

I can't believe that motherfucker hid not one but three fucking kids from me. What have I ever done to deserve some shit like this? I've done everything. I've cooked, cleaned, sucked, fucked and held him down. This is the thanks I get I thought to myself. I had really wanted to fuck some shit up back at the restaurant, but I wasn't going to give Chris the satisfaction of having me upset fuck him.

"Baby, I'm sorry I said that back there, I thought you knew about Samantha and their son," Javon apologized.

"No I didn't know, Javon. I also didn't know about Lauren and their five-year-old twins until last week. It's just so much I don't know; how could he have kept all of this from me? I don't whether to be sad or mad, but then again, our relationship was built on lies, so there is nothing that I should be sad about."

"Well baby, just know that lessons learned help you become a better person, and I'm here to help you better yourself, as long as you keep it 8 more them 92 with me," he replied." I was honestly feeling Javon, but I just wanted to take my time.

I knew that he didn't mean me no harm, but I also had to think about myself first, because I always put my man first, but I still got shitted on in the end. So from now on, it was about Marissa Gonzalez, and hopefully Javon Burns if he played his cards right; but I knew there was a lot more to him that he wasn't going to tell me, so I would have to figure it out, and possibly with the help of my girl Stasi, I swear she should've worked for the FBI that heffa finds out EVERYTHING and I mean everything.

JAVON

I can't believe that fuck boy played her like that? You get a good woman, yet you fuck around on her and hide your kids. I could never do no shit like that, I thought to myself. Yeah I fucked bitches, but that's all they were–bitches. They didn't do shit for me but suck and fuck, and I didn't give them shit but a slap on the ass and maybe a few dollars. Nobody could every say they saw me with a broad, because I only took them to this apartment I kept for them to come to. But Marissa? She could get any and everything she wanted; for some reason, I just had that feeling that she was "THE ONE," and now that I had her I wasn't going to let up, nor was I going to let my old hoes fuck up anything. I decided that as soon as Marissa left or went to sleep, I was letting every one of them know I was done. I would send them some cash for keeping it G with me, but that was all.

"Alright ma, we're here," I told her as we pulled up to my mini mansion. I had it built from the ground up. It was a 6-bedroom, 6-bathroom, four-level home with an elevator; 5,000 square feet of home, not including the 2,000 square feet of porch and balcony that surrounded the home.

"Damn Javon, this shit has nothing on anybody's house I've ever been to–well, besides Stasi's house," she explained. Although she didn't say anything, I could tell Marissa liked my house. I'm guessing she didn't want to seem like a groupie chick.

We walked inside. "What's mine is yours; make yourself at home, I'm about to run upstairs to run you a bath. There's some Patrón on the bar. Listen out for the intercom; I'll call you when I'm ready for you," I told her as I walked off. I decided to go ahead and shoot the text messages, because I didn't plan on letting her go home tonight.

ME: *I'm not going to be able to kick it with you anymore; I'm seeing somebody. Stop by the club to get some money. I appreciate you for always keeping it 100 with me*

Kay*: you must've texted the wrong person, I know you not trying to cut me off by text*

ME: *just come by the club we can talk then*

*

ME: *aye shawty, I'm not going to be able to fuck with you no more, it's been fun*

Ash*: that's some weak shit to text me instead of doing it in person, fuck you Jay.*

*

I watched Marissa from my surveillance footage that I had set up. I watched her fix a drink and then noticed that she was making me a drink as well. I can fuck with shawty for real. She thought about me and I didn't even ask. Any other chick would've fixed them several drinks and that's it; I guess that's what I had to remember, she wasn't anything like these other chicks out here.

"Come all the way upstairs to the fourth floor. It's the room on your right, and you can take the elevator. The elevator is one the second level on your left hand side. I announced over the intercom. Marissa followed my directions, and once the elevator stopped, I stood waiting on her.

"Hand me those drinks baby and follow me," I demanded, "I'm about to show you how you should be treated," I told her. I could tell once again that Marissa was in awe walking through my room. It was huge as hell. It was as if you were walking downstairs, with my room and my bathroom being the only thing on the fourth floor, it was spacious as hell. I had a living room set, a pool table, a California size bed and his and hers dressers. My room was red and black and manly, which was of course expected.

"Babe, you didn't have to do this," she whispered.

"I know I didn't, but I wanted you to know that's the difference between a man and a boy," I explained. I walked her into the bathroom, and I had candles and rose petals everywhere. I had a bottle of red wine chilled beside the Jacuzzi tub, ready for her. "I'm going to go ahead and give you some space; there's a TV to your left, and surround sound that you can hook up to your iPhone. The remotes are by the tub." I walked out, closing the door behind me and grabbing the Hennessy and Coke she had brought up to me.

"Damn, that girl knows the way to my heart," I chuckled.

I couldn't help but think back to the responses I got from those texts. I didn't want to hurt anyone, that's why I made sure I broke it off with them.

MARISSA

I undressed and couldn't believe that somebody did something like this for me. It was so thoughtless, but meant so much to me. I couldn't help it, but I wanted to cry. This was something I never ever experienced before.I just prayed that this wasn't something Javon was doing just to have sex cause that would be really fucked up. I thought about five years ago.

"*Dante, why don't you love me? What have I done to you to deserve this?" I cried hysterically to my boyfriend of three years.*

"You mean what can't you do, ma; you've had three miscarriages since we've been together. All I want is a child, and you can't seem to have my child, so why am I with you?" he shouted.

"I would expect you to be here with me, Dante, and not out fucking other bitches getting them pregnant. I'm out her stressing, worrying about you, and you leave me home alone to miscarry by myself– what type of shit is that?" I cried. All I wanted more than anything was to have kids, but with so much stress, I just couldn't make it past month two without miscarrying.

"Look, I don't want to be with you, alright? So quit calling me. I'm having a child with someone else!" he yelled, and stormed out of the apartment.

"Whyyyyyy!" I screamed; it was beyond devastating to me. I would've had three kids if it wasn't for him being out all night, not returning my calls, and not coming home. I had lost so much in the past three years that all I kept thinking about was ending it. My dad didn't want me and neither did a man. I just figured what is there to continue to live for? There wasn't a purpose. Maybe if I took a ton of pills, I would

finally be able to meet my kids in heaven. No, I'm better than that I yelled fuck Dante fuck my daddy fuck everybody I'm worth loving I cried I'm worth loving and their going to miss me when I'm gone.

I realized I was crying. Why is my sentimental ass crying? I laughed. I thought back to the miscarriages I had and prayed that God would answer my prayers and give me a man that wasn't so caught up in the street life and could be satisfied with me and only me.

*

JAVON

KNOCK KNOCK

"Yo Rissa, you good in there, baby? You been in there for almost two hours' baby; you ain't ready to get out?"

"I'm coming now babe, didn't realize it had been that long; give me a minute. Did you bring my clothes up?"

"Yeah I brought them up and put them in the dresser," I told her, not sure if she was going to cuss me out for doing that.

"Ok that's cool, I'm getting out now," she yelled. I listened to her let the water out of the tub, ready to see her and hold her and just be with her just in case she felt like this was it for us. I was sitting on the bed with just sweatpants on. I had been waiting for her to come out it seemed like forever, but I didn't want to keep rushing her.

"Feeling better baby? You were in there awhile."

"Yeah, I feel so much better, thank you so much," she told me. I pulled her to me and just held her; I couldn't help but smile this was something that I could get used to doing with her.

CASEY

We had just arrived back at my condo almost ten minutes ago, and I tried to wake Stasi up, but she was literally knocked out. *Fuck it, I might as well carry her up the stairs,* I thought. Soon as I got out and walked around to pick her up, she jumped up.

"OMG, I can't believe I fell asleep. I was really tired," she expressed.

"You good ma, I was just about to carry you to the crib," I laughed.

"You was not about to carry my fat ass, Casey; you would've dropped me quick, then I would've had to fight you," she laughed as she gathered her things. "I hope it's ok if I stay the night, I'm not trying to drive back to Jacksonville tonight."

"You good ma, I didn't plan on you leaving anyway." As we walked towards the building, Stasi told me that she had the eerie feeling again.

"Casey, you don't feel like we're being watched?" she asked.

"No, I feel like you're paranoid, 'Ms. Haitian Cartel'," I joked. She shook her head as we got on the elevator I guess I was going to learn real soon whether she was exactly who she said she was.

THE SPY

I had been following Stasi all day; I knew that me and her father had taught her better. I knew she felt someone watching, because I saw her look around several times.

RING RING!

"Mwen te jwenn deyò ki moun li te (I found out who he was)."

SILENCE

"non li se Casey (his name is Casey)."

SILENCE

"li te nan jwèt la dwòg depi li te katòz (he has been in the drug game since he was fourteen), he vini tounen pwòp (he comes back clean), li te fè yon chèk tou (she did a check also), men panse me li se sou m' (I think she is on to me)."

CLICK.

I couldn't believe Janeiro hung up on me, what type of shit is that I thought to myself. I can't believe he has me following her around; she has been in this game to long to slip; he should trust her.

"If she decides to keep this Casey guy around, we need to get his condo windows bulletproofed, as well as all his cars–that is, if he has more than one," I chuckled to myself. One would think that I would grow weary over following someone day in and day out, but when you were a protector, there was nothing you wouldn't do to make sure the person you were protecting was ok. I was about ready to get back to Haiti though, and wear regular clothes; right now, I was in all black–hoodie, hat, shirt, pants, and even my Timbs were black–and I know I was creeping people out with them not being able to see my face.

STASI

"I'm about to shower babe, I'll be ready to chill once I'm done," I yelled to Casey.

"Alright, I'll be in the guest bathroom taking a shower so we can chill," Casey yelled back. I watched him grab some polo pajamas pants and walked to the guest shower to handle his hygiene. *Man today has been one of the best I wonder what waking up to him is like* ,I thought to myself.

I hope my dad doesn't ruin this for me; this is the first guy I've given a try in years, and I really love it. I just have to make sure his head is on right before I help him become richer, and bring him into my world. *I wonder what he looks like naked; sheesh, 'cause he is one fine man*, I wondered. I knew Casey was probably wondering what I was doing? I heard him come in the room about 15 minutes ago. I knew what I was doing though he would be happy with what I was doing,I'm sure of it.

"Yo Stasi you good," Casey said as he opened the door. "Dddamn ma, my bad, I didn't expect you to still be naked," he said, but didn't stop staring.

"Well I know it's your house, but you could've knocked; what if I was on the toilet?" I said as I walked out the bathroom with one of his Polo Ralph Lauren towels wrapped around me, and walked into his bedroom.

"Then shit, you would've just been on the toilet; no harm no foul, ma. I want you comfortable around me," he told me as he walked behind me.

"Well I don't have no problem doing that," I whispered as I took my dreads out of the ponytail they were in, and my hair cascaded down to my ass. Casey just continued to stare, with his dick as hard as a rock.

"Ma, Imma let you handle your business in here. I'll be up front," he told me as he tried to turn to exit.

"Well, what if I wanted you to handle me, daddy?" I said. I licked my finger as I sat on his bed and spread my legs to start pleasing myself.

Was I nervous? Fuck no; I already knew that Casey wanted me from the moment he sent those drinks in Capones. I was so in tune with my sexuality that having sex with him right now didn't bother me. Also, I had done a deep background check on him–credit, insurance, doctor records, previous landlords, previous jobs–anything you could think of, I had it done. Casey turned around, and his dick wouldn't stop jumping

"Damn baby, you sure you ready for this?" he asked.

"I wouldn't be here right now if I wasn't Casey, now come fuck me and shut the fuck up," I demanded. It had been six long years; all I wanted was his dick deep within my walls. Before I could even finish the sentence, he was on me like white on rice. He was kissing me ever so gently and pulling my dreads. It had been so long for me, I couldn't take it. "Just fuck me"I said.

"Sssh ma, let me handle this, let me treat you right," he told me. He began to eat my pussy. He started off slow then he began to eat it faster.

"Oh yesssss baby yesssss!" I yelled. He inserted one finger, then two fingers. I was so spent I couldn't talk. He flipped me over, and then entered me; I could've sworn that his eyes started to cross.

“Fuck Stasi, this pussy so tight,” he said “Ughhhh yes, throw it back baby!” he shouted. He pulled my dreads up, so my face was next to his and kissed on me neck. “This pussy so good I’ve been trying not to cum to fast but it’s hard you wet as hell baby.”

“I'm about to come, Stasi. Come with me baby.” He pulled my hair one last time and we came together. I couldn’t move, I didn’t know if the sex was just really damn good or if he had wonderful dick or hell it could’ve been cause I ain’t had none in years. Whatever the case I was satisfied as hell...

JANEIRO

I just know that my daughter did not miss this meeting, what the heck could she be doing, I thought to myself. And where in the heck is my spy? He should've called me hours ago, I was starting to think the worst. If something happened to my child, I will paint the whole country red until I find out where me fucking child is.

RING RING RING! My phone begins to ring.

"Kisa ou vie? (what do you want?)?”

"m pa wè l' kite (I didn’t see her leave)," my spy told me. "

twouve l' byen (well find her),” I demanded before I disconnected the call.

"Jose, José come now."

"Yes sir,” José the butler said.

"Call another meeting ASAP with the entire Cartel. I need them here immediately," I was panicking I didn’t know what to do. This is not like my daughter. I seriously did not like going into the states, but for my child I was going with guns blazing, and an army ready to kill ANY and everything.

CHRIS

If Marissa thinks she's going to get off easy, she got another thing coming. That bitch had me in full jack-boy mode, and I didn't care what was going to come out of this. My mind was clouded due to being pissed off and a bit embarrassed, so revenge was the only thing I was seeing clear right now.

"Alright alright, shut the fuck up and listen up!" I yelled to my crew. "I have $55K for whoever can bring me my ex Marissa, unharmed and alive, no hair on her head touched. And another $80K for anyone that can bring me that pussy ass nigga Javon. I don't give a fuck if he is dead or alive, just get him to me. Now get the fuck out of here and find one or both of them TODAY, and don't waste my fucking time."

This was going to be so fun; I can't wait, man. Just thinking about what was going to happen was making my dick rock hard, and I just couldn't stop smiling. Killing people or even hurting them turned me on. I used to kill squirrels when I was younger just to get hard, and then go fuck something. My friends thought it was weird, but I didn't think anything was wrong with it. To me, it was just like getting hard every time you see your chick. Your hard dick expresses your love for her.

MARCUS

Ring Ring Ring!

"Listen real quick, you don't have to say anything, just listen," I whispered. "Remember you told me to get in good with the nigga Chris' crew to find out if he was going to try and retaliate on you? Well today is our lucky day; he just put a hit out on you and your girl," I informed him excitedly.

When it came down to the murder game, I was definitely the one you would call on. I had been murkin' niggas since I was 12 years old. Back in the day, some nigga who thought he was "the man" and wanted to impress his crew by stealing my brand new Jordans was my first kill. He stole my Jordans and left me to walk 12 miles all the way back home; so the next day, I waited on him to walk out of his house to get ready to go to school. I blew his brains out right in front of his moms, then I killed her, snatched my shoes off his feet, and went to school. Crazy as it may sound, I wasn't scared back then, and now I'm the one everyone calls when they have a problem.

"This nigga really think he can put a bounty on my head for real man? He got the game all the way fucked up, let's show him who he playing with, Marcus. I want a $3 million cash bounty put on him, and I want him ALIVE!" Javon yelled.

"You got it bruh, I'm putting the word out as we speak," I advised before I hung up.

Three million? Three fucking million? Yeah, my boy got that cash man," I said out loud. I was just excited for the kill. I didn't need the money by a long shot, but my young bulls were most definitely going to be raging to get out and get that money. I loved to see my young niggas eat, because these days motherfuckers didn't take care of their crew; that's why they turned on them or tried to take over.

JAVON

This motherfucker think he can put a bounty on me and my girl head and live? He got me fucked up man, I thought to myself. I don't understand why he's so upset that I'm doing what he didn't want to with Marissa, and now he wants to harm her–what type of fuck shit is that, man? I was beyond pissed. I never knew what it was like to disrespect a woman that I cared for, because I had never done it, and would never do it.

My motto was YOU REAP WHAT YOU SOW, and I believed it to the fullest extent; that was another reason why I was so hell bent on doing the right thing and getting out of the game fully–shit was sweet when you hadn't gotten caught, but you never knew when someone was going to snitch on you, or try to kill you because they were tired of being in the shadows. I didn't want my wife and kids looking over their shoulders all the time, or even worse, being killed because someone was trying to get back at me. I knew that Casey would never go fully legit, no matter what. He only went in on the club just so that he could keep the cops at bay with his income, showing that he was actually making legit money by the return that the club brought in every night.

I had to get out the game. I had a degree, and I wasn't even using it to the fullest extent. *I'm just basically wasting my talents* I thought.. I won't lie to myself and say I don't have talents in the street, because I did and I could tell the way I was and had been dominating the drug game. . I knew I had talents to be as great as any known major drug dealer, but I didn't want everything that came with it. I just wanted to be able to never worry about where my next dollar was coming from. As long as I had my businesses open and all my money overseas, I was good for as long as I lived.

STASI

“Oh my God, oh my God!” I yelled as I jumped up. “What time is it, Casey?”

“It's ummm, it's 10 a.m. ma–why, what's wrong,” Casey said, confused.

"My dad is going to fucking kill me, man. OMG OMG, I can’t believe I overslept, fuck!”

“Babe just calm down, it can't be that serious, like what's the worst that could happen?” he asked.

“You don't know my fucking dad, Casey. I was supposed to be in Haiti at 6 a.m., and it is 10 a.m. My father has had time to assemble a meeting, call his crew, and be in the states by now–fuck fuck fuck!” I yelled as I scrambled to gather some clothes. “Look, I’m going to leave this stuff here, I will be back sometime tonight; if not tonight, then it will be tomorrow. I will text you when I can,” I said as I headed to the door. "Who in the f," I said as I opened the door.

"Well my child, I see that all is well with you. I am just trying to understand why you were not in Haiti for the meeting this morning at 6, and why in the fuck am I here, Stasi? You know I'm not supposed to ever step foot in the States,” my father demanded.

"Papa, I’m sorry. I overslept and my phone was still on silent from yesterday when we were at the theme park. I'm so sorry.”

“Well we must go, the families are waiting; you know that I don't hesitate to make calls when I cannot reach you,” my father said as he held his hand out.

JANEIRO

"You will have no time to change. We are heading to the jet so we can get this meeting started; you have people trying to pay us millions of fucking dollars, and you're laid up with some nigga." I was beyond furious–not because she met a man, but because she missed a very important meeting. I had decided to step back and let her handle everything, and I didn't want nor need her fucking up to where everyone thought she was a joke, and wouldn't ever take her serious.

"Do you have all the numbers everyone owes us, Stasi?"

"Yes Papa, I have everything; it was a simple mistake. I swear it won't happen again," she murmured honestly.

"Good, because I would hate for you to have to move back to Haiti with me to ensure that you would be on time every time there is a meeting." I hated to be a hard ass, but I had been molding her for this, and I didn't want her to lose focus on what was important. I also just wanted her to be safe and understand that not everyone had her best interest, so she couldn't be so easy to give.

MARCUS

"Alright, so Jay put a million-dollar bounty on Chris's head and he wants him ALIVE. He's talking hardcore cash in your hands, so don't fuck this up. This could put you on Jay's roster as one of his gunman," I announced to the crew.

"A million dollars." Everyone just kept repeating it to make sure they heard correctly. I really didn't give a damn about the money; I just wanted to see Chris dead and make sure my people were safe from his dumb ass–that's it. I decided if Chris was going to hide, then I was going to get the next best thing to lure him out and that was his mother and kids.

I hopped in my rental truck that I decided to get since I was playing "detective" for Javon. I headed towards the westside to Eureka Gardens, where I was praying Chris' mother and kids were. With no actual plan in mind, I pulled up to her apartment and lucky for me, Chris was stupid enough to trust me early on and had already introduced me to his mother. I knocked on the door, and Chris's mother answered.

"Hey Miles, how are you baby, what's going on?" she asked.

"Hey Ms. Williams, Chris told me to come get you and the kids; there is a bounty on his head, and he wants you all hidden so no one tries to harm you guys in order to get at him."

"I don't know why that motherfucker can't leave people alone. I'm too old for this shit. Ok, let me get us some bags, Miles." I was glad I never told them my real name; I never used my real cellphone, and never drove my actual car. This was going to work perfect, because nobody knew the real deal about me. I couldn't help but smile at how easy this was, and how stupid and gullible Chris was; it was pitiful.

"Alright, I got everything; grab their car seats and let's get the fuck out of dodge!" Ms. Williams yelled. I grabbed their car seats and put them in my Tahoe rental.

"Ms. Williams, this truck has 4G LTE if you want to use the Internet while we are driving." I didn't quite know what I was going to do with all of them yet, but I would have a plan soon enough.

CASEY

Damn I can't believe she wasn't lying; I'm fucking with a modern day queen pin. How could she hide that shit from people for all these years? It actually turned me on a little bit, but then again, I didn't want her to think she ever had to put me on. I wanted her to know I would work for everything, but all in all, I was with her for her–fuck what she could potentially do for me. I also felt that I had to protect her more than ever now; knowing that her dad wasn't always in the states, I don't want anyone thinking they could use that to their advantage.

I might as well go ahead and get dressed and get to this money until my baby gets back. I was elated she was giving me a chance, and I was going to make it worth her while. I decided on some all-red Robin jeans, a regular white t-shirt, and my favorite shoes, which were cherry Jordan 13s, and headed out the door. I hopped in my black on black Dodge Charger, and headed to the north side to see what was going on.

Riding down Moncrief, I was flagged down by one of my workers, so I pulled over in Winn Dixie's parking lot.

"Yo Casey, you heard about the boun–"

POP…POP…POP!

"Yo, what the fuck, who's shooting at us?" I hopped in my car, and lucky for me, it was bulletproof. I grabbed my bulletproof vest and my MK-16 with extended clip, and started shooting the car that was headed directly for us

ZAT… ZAT… ZATTTTTTTTTTTTTTTTTTT.

I was able to shoot the driver and the passenger that was hanging out the window trying to shoot at us; their car swerved and flipped over three times.

"Fuck, get in your car and get the fuck out of here, I don't know what this was, but we ain't taking the wrap, let's go!" I yelled to the worker, closing the door to my charger and heading towards Javon's house.

MARISSA

Ugh nobody wants to tell me anything about Javon. They can't be that scared of him. This was going to be way harder to find out then I intentionally thought. I had called everyone that I knew that also knew Javon, and all they would tell me was he was a good man, and also the owner of Capones, which of course I already knew. *I wonder where the fuck Stasi is, I haven't heard from that hoe in days.* I decided to text my friend and see what was going on with her.

ME: dónde estás (where are you)

Stasi: con papa en haití (with papa in haiti)

ME: ¿ por qué coño (what the fuck why)

Stasi: me perdí la reunión de esta mañana (I missed the meeting this morning)

ME: wow qué estés jodiendo (wow you're fucking up)

Stasi: no I'm no fue un error (no I'm not it was one mistake)

ME: te amo tener cuidado (love you be careful)

Stasi: también te amo (love you too)

My next step was to see if Javon was going to tell me about this bounty supposedly on our heads. After all the reevaluating I had done on my life, I decided it was time to finish my degree; although I would never admit it to anyone, I wanted to be successful just like Stasi. I sort of looked up to my best friend, even though she was younger than me. She was so outspoken as well as feisty; she didn't put up with any shit, and I loved that about her. I had finally decided to get off my ass and see how many credits I needed to obtain my associate's degree in health business administration. I was kind of excited and ready to take the world by storm; no man was going to keep me down anymore.

I rushed to throw on a Victoria's Secret pink outfit, my favorite Ugg boots, and then I grabbed my transcripts, iPad, and iPhone, and ran to my car. I was headed towards Florida State Community College at Jacksonville.

CHRIS

Man why the fuck isn't my moms answering the phone? Man what the fuck is she doing? I wondered what my mom could be doing with all three of my kids with her?

RING RING RING!

"What you want, Chris?" Lauren asked.

"Quit acting like a fucking brat right now. Did you take the twins from my mom's house?" I asked her.

"No you fucking idiot, the kids were still there to my knowledge, what the fuck is going on, Chris?" Lauren asked.

"You think if I fucking knew I would be calling your dumb ass? NO! So kiss my ass, you dumb bitch. I'll figure it out without your stupid ass," I shouted as I hung up.

RING RING RING!

"Yes sir, how can I help you? Chris Jr. wasn't supposed to be back until Friday, so why you bothering me?" Samantha demanded.

“ I take it your ass didn't come get Jr. early. I'm trying to figure out where him, the girls, and my mom are.”

“Well they ain't in my pocket, stop worrying and leave me alone; if they were in trouble, your mom would've let you know!” Samantha yelled and hung up. *Dumb bitches get on my fucking nerves, like why in the fuck did I ever mess with either one of they dumb asses* I thought to myself. I decided to call Miles to get him to see if he could figure something out.

RING RING RING!

“What's happening playa?” Marcus answered.

“Miles, I need a favor, man. I need you to ride past my mom’s apartment and see what the fuck is going on, she isn't answering her phone.”

“Iight man, I got you, chill out. I'm pretty sure she chilling with the kids, it's nothing to worry about, man,” Marcus said.

“Yeah, I know I'm probably overreacting just hit me back as soon as you find out something, alright? Oh, and I appreciate it,” I said before hanging up. Something didn’t feel right, and I didn't give a fuck how long it took, I would body any and every fucking nigga over my kids and mom–for real man, this shit was getting to me. If I didn't care about anything, my kids as well as my mom were my hearts.

STASI

"Alright, gentlemen. I would like to apologize for my tardiness this morning. I would also like to reassure you it will not happen again," I announced. "Now, on to the business at hand. Jiménz family, we just want to thank you for all you have done the past month in Colombia, but we do expect a lot more from you, and soon. This month we have upped your supply, so you will have 110 keys; you will owe us $1.9 million by September 12th. That gives you exactly one month to show us that you are worth something to this organization."

"Rasmussen family, you have done a great job with all your crews in Europe. We have upped your keys an extra 200 keys, making it a total of 1,000 keys, because we know you can handle it. Your ticket will be $10 million come September 12th. Do you think that you can handle this?" I asked, already knowing the answer.

"We most definitely can handle it, and we thank you for trusting us; we won't let you down," the head of the Rasmussen family said proudly.

"Great! Now on to the Arpasi family; you have done an ok job. I know the loss of a few of your workers has slowed you down. However, you went from 1,000 keys a month to 350 keys; you're in the hole $5.2 million, and we need that ON TIME next month–no more handouts, no more half-ass work. If you can't live up, then we will select a new family to market us in Peru. This is your final warning," I stressed.

"Le'Roux family in Paris–excellent work; you have added 200 more keys, totaling 450 keys. Your ticket is $5.8 million due September 12th. Patel family in Asia, awesome fucking job. I'm proud of you guys;

875 keys, your ticket is 12.6 million. Do we have any questions and or concerns at this time?" I asked everyone as I looked around the table.

Everyone looked around, but said nothing. I could tell the Jiménz and Arpasi families were visibly upset, but it was what it was. I wasn't going to continue to let them think that it was ok to not bring much in when we had plenty of motherfuckers that could really bring us money.

"Alrighty, well since we are all on the same page, you all know your drop off locations and times. Remember, cash must be counted, and mistakes will be reprimanded, got it?"

"Got it," they said in unison.

"I will need the head of the Arpasi and Jiménz families to stay behind–everyone else, you are more than welcome to stay for dinner, and we will see you again in one month. Be safe and remember, 'all is fair in love and drugs'."

Everyone exited and retreated to the mansion, where we always entertained the families; there was liquor, women, weed, and pills. We didn't allow anyone to do cocaine, because my father figured if they did it in front of us, what would stop them hide and do it, or better yet take from our product?

"Mr. Jiménz, we know that we have just upped you to 110 keys, and that you are progressing more and more; however, we want you to understand that you are the only ones not selling enough to be profitable. So that we have everything clear, we need you to know that by next month, you would need to be ready to move at least 400 keys, or we or we are going to have to terminate this business," I spoke sternly and kept eye contact.

"No no, we understand and we will be more than ready. Our families have been connected for years and we cannot let this partnership go down the drain; we will pick up more and thank you for the opportunity Mademoiselle Boudreaux," Mr. Jiménz spoke.

"Great, you may join the party, thank you for coming Mr. Jiménz. Now to you, Mr. Arpasi. I want to say this as clear as fucking possible," I said as I turned towards him with my silenced Tiffany blue 9. "If you continue to fuck with me or my money, we will have a big fucking problem. First off, how in the fuck do you go from 1K keys to 350? What the fuck is going on in Peru? Do I need to send someone to fucking look over your shoulder like a child?" I was beyond livid.

"Nnnnnno, Ms. Boudreaux, no one is messing with your money, everything is fine, very sorry, it won't happen again," he stammered.

"I don't give a fuck; as of right now, you are indebted to me 10 million PLUS the 5.2 million for next month–no more fucking excuses, now get the fuck out of here," I said as I shooed him.

"Ou konnen li can't fè konfyans (you know he can't be trusted)," my father asked.

"Mwen konnen papa (I know papa)," I sighed.

"Ou okipe tèt ou gwo I'm trè fyè (you handled yourself well I'm very proud)," my father announced.

"Di ou mèsi anpil papa (thank you so much papa)," I cried. All I ever wanted was to make my father proud, and now I knew that that was exactly what I was doing.

MARCUS

“Hey Miles, what did my son want?” Ms. Williams asked.

“Oh he wanted me to let you and the twins know you needed to throw out your iPhones, because someone can try and track us that way, and he wanted to make sure that we weren't in any type of harms way,” I told her.

“Oh hell no–twins, give me your phones now right now!” Ms. Williams yelled. She grabbed the phones and smashed them to pieces.

“This is some bullshit, who’s going to pay for new phones? I need a phone to play candy crush on,” Ms. Williams told me.

“Ok, I got y’all, you just have to promise me you will only play games–no texting, no emailing, no calling anyone, because that could put us in danger. Do we have an agreement?” I asked sternly.

“Yes we have an agreement,” the twins and Ms. Williams yelled.

“Alright cool, let’s go get y’all some new phones, some clothes, some food, and toiletries; there's no telling how long we are going to be here.” I was happy that I didn’t tell them my real name and I never drove my real car around them. It was always rentals. It would take Chris and his clan of retards to find out who I really was.

I had decided to take them to Savannah, Georgia to my duck off house that I had in the Landmark Historic district that only myself, Javon, and Casey knew about. It was a roomy 5-bedroom, 4.5-bedroom house that slept 12 comfortably. It was equipped with toys and games. I always kept it stocked for times like this, because I never knew what could happen or when I would just need a getaway.

Myself, Ms. Williams, and the kids headed for my rental, and then headed to find a T-Mobile. We ended up finding a T-Mobile on Martin Luther King Jr. Blvd.

"Ms. Williams, here's some money, go ahead inside and get you and the twins whatever you want–iPhones, iPads, whatever, just do not, I repeat do not call anyone. I'll be out here in the truck. I have a few calls I need to make; let me know if you need more money."

"Ok baby, we'll spend your little money happily; see you in a bit." Once I saw that they had walked into T-Mobile, I pulled out my other phone to text Javon and give him the run-down.

ME: yo Von, I got them out at the spot

Von: bet, everything good out there?

ME: everything 100, their phones are gone, I'm in the rental, and I got them getting new phones as we speak

Von: cool, I'll give you whatever y'all spend back. I know you not pressed about it, but I gotta give it back, just feels right since you doing this for me

ME: 10/4, keep me posted on what's on the up and up

Von: 10/4, be safe

ME: Fasho

As soon as I got done, I happened to look up just in time, because Ms. Williams was coming out of the store with the kids in tow and a few bags. As soon as they got in the truck, she started rambling.

"I hope you don't mind, I got all of us iPhones and iPads, and I got junior a tablet so he wouldn't be bugging the girls the entire time, since we don't know how long we are going to be here," she said wide eyed.

"I don't mind, Ms. Williams, just give me the receipts, everything is cool, I promise," I assured her. What she didn't know was her son was going to eventually pay for all of this with his death.

JAVON

I wonder where Rissa ass is? I haven't heard from her ass all day where the hell her ass at ?I thought.

KNOCK KNOCK…

Who the fuck could that be? Nobody knew where I lived but a few people, and they always called me first.

"Who the fuck is it!" I yelled. There was no answer, so I grabbed my gun as I walked towards the door. I didn't look out the peephole, just in case somebody had a gun or some shit there ready to blow my mind. I peeked out the window that was next to the front door, but I didn't see anybody.

"Man, I don't have time for games, I said who the fuck is it!" I snapped as I yanked open the door. "Damn, what's up Rissa? I was just thinking about you, why you didn't tell me you was coming, ma? You had me about to shoot up the door," I chuckled.

"Would this have been before or after you told me that there was a fucking bounty on my head, Von? You got me out here walking blind, and that shit is not cool at all," she shook her head.

"Baby I promise you, I'm working on that as we speak. The nigga's biggest mistake he ever made was placing a bounty on your head and thinking the shit was cool," I yelled.

"Well I appreciate that very much Von, I really do; it hurts that this motherfucker could even fix his lips to put a fucking hit out on me. I want him delivered to me–fuck anybody else, because I've been through the most hurt out of anyone!" she yelled.

"I got you ma, I promise we will hand deliver him to you, and you can handle his ass, straight up," I assured her.

"Great, now the main reason I came was to tell you some great news," she smiled.

"Well, you can't be pregnant because we haven't had sex yet, so tell me, what is the second best news you could give me," I said as I picked her up.

"Well baby, I went by Florida State College at Jacksonville to see how many credits I needed for my associates degree in Health Business Administration, and it was only two damn credits," she started laughing. "Ain't that some shit?"

"Well that's great ma, how long is it going to take before you're done?"

"Two damn months," she said, furious. "I could've been done, but I let people cloud my judgment, but it's cool and it's over. I start on Monday."

"Well it looks like we have a reason to shop, let's go baby," I laughed. "Let me run upstairs real fast and put on some clothes. I was going to bum around the house today."

I ran upstairs to throw on some clothes. I had my music blasting, and my projector screen had my NBA 2K15 career profile up; I was just about to start my season. I decided on some grey Levi 501s, a white Nautica shirt, and my all-white Nike Roshe. Babe, I think your phone is ringing!" Marissa yelled.

CASEY

"Why the fuck isn't Von answering his fucking phone? "I said to myself as he hung up for the 5th time. Let me just text this slow ass nigga.

ME: Von what the fuck are you doing man, 911, answer yo fucking phone

Von: I didn't have service bruh, what's wrong

ME: I was just shot at, I'm almost to your crib, open the garage man

Von: 10/4, I was just about to leave with my girl, I'll be downstairs

ME: Bet

These niggas shooting at me must've thought Von was with me, but they don't know they just signed their death certificate. I pulled into Javon's garage and closed it behind me.

"Sak pase, my friend," Javon said as I walked in the house.

"M'ap lite (I'm alive,") I murmured.

"Tell me what the fuck happened bruh, you telling me niggas shooting at you in broad daylight, man?" Javon asked.

"Iight, so I'm cruising down Moncrief and one of the youngins flagged me down, so we both pull over in the Winn-Dixie parking lot, and as soon as we was about to talk, motherfuckers just started shooting at us; luckily I was in my Charger or I swear, I'd be dead," I replied.

“Damn, they must have thought that my Charger was your Charger, damn man, I’m sorry. I’m glad you’re ok, I don’t know what the fuck I would do without you, bruh,” Javon told me.

“On another note bruh, let me tell you some crazy shit. Alright, so Stasi stays at my house last night; she over sleeps, and guess who shows up this morning,” I said. “The fucking head of the Haitian Cartel man, like my future girl is big shit, so I don't think she would even be interested in me for real,” I announced. “My girl likes you Cas, otherwise she wouldn’t have even hung with you yesterday, nor stayed at your crib overnight. Believe me, if she let you find out who she really really is, she likes you and I'm being 100% honest,” Marissa explained.

“I just don't understand why she would want to be with me if she has it all,” I said to Marissa.

“It's not about having it all, it’s about not having love; money doesn't mean everything to Stasi,” Marissa explained as she walked to the living room. Maybe she's right man, maybe she's right. I just don't know I don't want to get my hopes up, man.

THE SPY

This boy has got to be an idiot; he has not checked his surroundings not once. I've been following him for days, then he gets shot at and still he hasn't checked his surroundings at all–he can't be serious. I decided it was time to go ahead and check in since it didn't look like anything was going to change.

ME: li pa te tcheke anviwonman I (he has not checked his surroundings)

Boss: nenpot lot bagay (anything else)

ME: li te tire nan jodi a te kaoab dwe fe ere idantite ant l ak Wobe (he was shot at today, could be mistaken identity between him and javon)

The spy was so busy looking down at his phone that he didn't see Casey walk up to his car, which he thought was hidden pretty well.

CLICK CLICK

"Well well, first things first, who the fuck is your boss, and why the fuck have you been following me?" Casey grilled as he pressed his gun to my head.

"My boss is Mr. Boudreaux, therefore, I have been following you to ensure that you are able to provide the safety to Ms. Boudreaux that her father feels she needs before he puts his trust in you, and before he allows her to come back to the States. If he feels that you are not capable of providing her safety, then you will no longer be able to contact her again."

“To go ahead and make you aware, I’ve known you’ve been following us since we were in Orlando at the mall; you followed us to my condo. I wanted to say something, but Stasi somehow knew everything was ok.”

I picked up my phone to go ahead and text my boss again to let him know what was up.

*

ME: He actually did know I was following them, he told me what I was wearing and all

Boss: great I will allow her to come back home that was all I needed to know

ME: ok I will be headed back

*

“Now since you have been following me all day, did you see who the fuck shot at me earlier?” Casey asked me.

“Well now that you know who I am, can you take the damn gun away from my head? I'm not sure how you expect me to tell you something and you got a damn gun pressed to my head the entire time.”

“Oh my bad, I gotcha, just couldn’t be to sure,” Casey apologized.

“Ok so there was a meeting of people at the Winn-Dixie about 10 minutes before you pulled up; they were passing around pictures of cars, which I would guess it was yours, or maybe Javon’s since both your cars look the same. Of course, you know Chris is out for blood because he can't find his mother,” I explained.

"Man you know a lot of shit, what's your name?" Casey asked.

"That I am not ready to disclose, but no worries, you will find out soon enough. Now if you don't mind, I must be on my way to the jet so that I can get to Haiti before Stasi arrives back; if you need me, here is my number. Don't hesitate to give me a call," I told him as I handed him a card and started up my car. *He might just be what she needs after all*, I thought. Hopefully he is able to handle what comes with being in the Haitian Cartel; if not, he will have to relocate.

JANEIRO

"Alright my child, I can now stop holding you hostage, even though I love you being here. I only held you to make sure Casey was on the up and up before I allowed him to continue to live and be in your life," I advised my daughter.

"Papa, you think I didn't know you had someone following us? You're my father; I may know your next move before you do. I love you and thank you for always protecting me. I'll be back early next month to do some pop up pickups," Stasi told me as she kissed me.

I just couldn't believe my daughter didn't want to stay in Haiti. I knew she hated it here, but I missed her being here with me, but it was like after the loss of her mother, she just became so fascinated with living in the States. Although I would never force her to stay, I loved threatening her with the possibility.

"Just know that I'm always three steps ahead of you until I feel like I can trust him wholeheartedly," I warned her. I went ahead and made plans for the jet to be prepared to take off as soon as she arrived. I also had to make sure that my spy knew to come back to Haiti in a few days. I didn't know what I would do if something happened to my daughter. I think that's why I was so overprotective; losing my wife and son just ruined me completely.

CHRIS

“This shit ain't making no sense, where is my mother and kids!” I yelled as I punched the wall. Nobody had no explanation of how my mother and my three kids just all of a sudden vanished at the blink of an eye. I just couldn't figure out why someone would take my mother and kids. I guess that the *no women and kids* rule didn't apply to everyone these days. I also didn't understand why the fuck their phones were now disconnected; they just disappeared in a matter of twelve hours.

“I don't care what you do, I know somebody better find them, or people are about to start dropping like flies. Matter of fact, you know the spot on Edgewood and Lem Turner where Jay’s people hang out? I want y'all to go shoot it up, and I don’t give a fuck who gets hit; if they're out there, they get hit. Hope they got insurance to cover funerals,” I chuckled. My crew filed out of the warehouse and headed towards Jay’s crew spot. I was praying for some good news as well as some major damage done. You fuck with my family, I fuck with everything you have that you think is untouchable, starting with your crew.

MEANWHILE IN THE CAR (MELVIN)

Being Chris' right hand man, I was looked at to take charge in this.

"Alright everybody, it's do or fucking die right now," I said. I was nervous somewhat, because I wasn't into just shooting random folks, and it made it a little hard that they didn't do anything. Chris didn't understand he was about to start a war that we weren't equipped for, but my man was in a hard spot because somebody had the balls to possibly kidnap his family.

As the car turned on Edgewood, everybody masked up. Thankfully, it was after 9 p.m., so there were no kids were out.

"Light it up," I told them.

ZAT...ZAT...POP...POP...ERKKKKKKK...

We peeled off as quick as we had come. I was absolutely pleased there were no kids outside. I can't believe them niggas was just standing out there with no knowledge of their surroundings. How you call yourself a dope, boy but you just got caught slipping?

"Get to the spot and hurry up," I reminded them; it was time for reminiscing.

We got back to the warehouse fairly quickly; the young boys were ready to fill Chris in on what went down. I had to remind them we needed to get rid of the weapons and the stolen car. I had two of them take the stolen car underneath the Dames Point bridge, and set the car on fire. I took all their guns and started taking the bullets out, then I dumped all of the guns in a barrel of acid so there would be no trace of the guns ever. I know they probably didn't give a fuck if they got caught, but I damn sure did.

STASI

"I need this jet back in Jacksonville within the hour, no excuses, do you understand me?" I questioned the pilot.

I pulled out all three of my iPhones and looked to see if I had any missed calls or texts. None. Damn, don't nobody love me, and where is Casey's ass at? I ain't heard from my boo in a minute, what is really going on? I decided to call my assistant and see how everything was going at the office.

RING RING RING

"Hello, thank you for calling Boudreaux and Associates, this is Kaylen, how may I direct your call?"

"Kaylen, how are you today, this is Stasi. I was calling to see if you have any news for me?" I questioned.

"Oh hey Stasi, I do have a few things to tell you," Kaylen announced. "Well, you had two hundred white roses delivered between yesterday and today, your two cases that you were waiting on the verdict from have come in, and some guy named Casey has called here over thirty times asking me when would you be back," Kaylen concluded.

"Ok Kaylen, you can leave the verdicts on my desk; if I'm not there this afternoon, I will be there bright and early in the morning. Also, if anyone else calls for me, take a message. Thank you for all you do, have a good day and thanks again," I acknowledged.

I was a little bit happier knowing Casey had been calling my office looking for me. I decided to set up a meeting with the heads of the five families to go over some business. I felt that it was time to let some people go for good. I had checked the halfway numbers from a few of them, and they were shit. I picked up my illegal business phone and sent the mass text to all the heads of the families.

*

ME: Meeting heads of families ONLY in 4 days same place

JIMÉNZ: see you soon

RASMUSSEN: great, have a issue to discuss

ARPASI: K

LE'ROUX: great

PATEL: awesome

*

Before I knew it, I was landing, but something didn't look right. "Why in the fuck are there police cars here? Did you do anything you weren't supposed to back there?" I quizzed the pilot.

"No ma'am, I got an ok to land and everything. I didn't do anything wrong," he exclaimed.

"Well hurry up and open the doors so I can see what the fuck they want." The pilot hurried and opened the door, and proceeded to let me out of the jet. I put on my Versace shades and headed towards the line of police waiting.

"Ma'am we would li–"

"If you're not the boss, shut the fuck up and get me the boss, you're wasting my time, and I would really love a shower," I demanded.

"Ma'am my name is Lieutenant Davenport, we would like to take you downtown to ask you some questions," he stated.

“Am I under arrest?” I asked

“No ma'am, you’re not, well not yet anyway,” he answered.

“Well until I'm under arrest, get all these dumb fucks away from me. I have business to tend to!” I yelled.

“Ms. Boudreaux,” he grabbed my arm, “We just ask for a moment of your time.” I spun around so fast you would think you saw my head spin.

“If you ever in your life put your hands on me, I will personally cut off your dick and shove it up your ass, while I talk to your captain and let him know that you are harassing me. Find you somebody else to harass, you fucking idiot because if not, we're going to have a big damn problem,” I threatened as I spun back around and walked to my waiting town car. “Who the fuck does he think he!” is I shouted. *Motherfucker don't know he just put his hand on the wrong person toda, I thought to myself.*

“Say bye bye to your career lieutenant because, when I'm finished you are going to wish you left me the fuck alone.” I yelled as I shot the detective a bird.

MARCUS

“Alright Ms. Williams, I have some bad news for you,” I told her.

“Oh no, is it Chris?” she panicked.

“No ma'am, it's not about him; it's about you, the kids, and this situation your son has gotten you in,” I told her.

"Well what about it? I figured we're going to be here for a while," she spoke honestly.

"Well Chris just called and told me that we need to be here for about a month or so. I have to meet with him to handle some things," I advised her.

"Well that's fine, you have cable, I'm loving my iPad, and the kids are happy. We just need more food, some snacks, and more towels so they can get in the pool," she rambled.

"Yes ma'am, I'll be sure to get everything that you guys need, just make sure you make no calls whatsoever. I'll be back shortly," I advised as I headed out the door.

RING RING RING!

"Chris, this Miles, what's going on?" I asked.

"My dude, where the fuck have you been? I haven't heard from you since yesterday. What the fuck you got going on that you can't call and tell me if you found my mom and kids, nigga?" Chris inquired.

"Look here, you my man and all, but I'm going to need you to watch how you talk to me," I snapped.

"Look my man, I don't give a fuck what you talking about man, if you ain't found my family yet, we gon' have some problems!" Chris yelled.

"Alright nigga, it's nothing, be ready," I hung up. *I don't know who this motherfucker thinks he is but he definitely picked the right fucking person to play with* I thought to myself. I decided to go ahead and head to Javon's cousin Tej's car shop called Murks. I decided to have Casey meet me at Murks, so I went ahead and texted him.

ME: Yo, meet at Murks off 3rd and Odessa

CASEY: 10/4, I'm in route

ME: bet, see you in a minute

I pulled up to Murks and was happy to see that the shop was almost finished being rebuilt. A few months ago, it was blown up, but I knew Tej wasn't going to stop pushing until it was rebuilt, and now it was almost finished. I walked in to see if Tej was in.

"Hey, is Tej in today?" I asked the receptionist.

"He not too long ago went to the store, he should be back any minute," she advised me.

"Alright bet," I said as I walked back outside to wait. As I walked out, Casey was pulling up.

"What's up bruh, how you living?" Casey asked me as he dapped me up.

"I'm good bruh, just trying not to kill Chris. I don't know who this nigga thinks he is, but I got his ass now. His mom thinks that they're in danger, so she ain't gon' call, and I got them out at my crib, so they good–at least, until he try some bullshit.

"Bet, well we definitely going to handle that for sure," Casey advised me.

MARISSA

I can't believe that Javon forgot I was here,I thought to myself as I headed towards the garage to my truck. I had decided I might as well go to the mall with Javon's black card. I drove towards the Avenues Mall so that I could find something to wear to Pure Saturday night, and being that it was already Thursday, I was late as hell trying to find something. I had my hair up in a messy bun. I had decided on a grey sundress, along with grey chucks, and I had decided to keep it as simple as possible as I walked around the big ass mall. I decided to go ahead and hit up Stasi and see if she wanted to meet me for a day of shopping.

RING RING RING

"Hey baby girl, what's up?" Stasi answered.

"Hey boo, I wanted to know if you were close to the avenues, and if you wanted to meet me. I'm here, but you know I shop the best with my ride or die chick," I laughed.

"Girl yeah, me and Kaylen were actually on the way there to shop and have lunch, we definitely can join you," Stasi announced.

"Good, I'll be waiting in the food court for you," I advised Stasi. I decided to go ahead and text Javon and let him know I had his card. I didn't want him thinking that I stole it or something.

*

ME: Hey baby, just wanted to let you know that I have your card, and I'm at the avenues about to shop with Stasi and Kaylen.

BOO: I know you got the card ma, but I'm guessing you didn't look at the name on the card.

ME: Huh?

BOO: Look at the card, Rissa

I looked down at the card and was shocked as hell that it had my name on it.

ME: when did you do that?

BOO: Doesn't matter, I told you what's mine is yours, so spend whatever, it's no pressure on it baby, have fun.

ME: Thank you so much baby

BOO: You welcome baby, see you later

*

I couldn't wait to show Stasi and Kaylen what Javon had done. For some reason, it felt like someone was watching me. I looked around, but I didn't notice anything out of the ordinary; that's strange as fuck. I decided to go ahead and get up; Stasi and Kaylen's butts were finally here.

"Hey girls, I missed y'all," I squealed as I hugged Stasi and Kaylen.

Every time we went somewhere as a trio, we had nothing but hating ass females staring at us, giving us dirty looks. I mean, I can't deny it, we all were baddies, and we couldn't help that their men stared at us instead of them; they couldn't be made at us. Kaylen was 5'9 and had big breasts and a perfect-shaped apple ass; she had long, bra-length hair that was all hers, and she had this lovely Jamaican accent that drove the boys wild. Her and Stasi both got the attention because of their accents; I was just the almost-thick Puerto Rican that hung out with them. I wouldn't say my self-esteem was low; I guess I just wanted to be looked at first instead of after them.

"Hey girl," Stasi and Kaylen said.

"Alright, y'all not going to believe what just happened to me," I quizzed them. Before they could even ask what, I started to ramble off.

"Von gave me my very own black card, and told me to spend whatever I wanted." I couldn't help but smile.

"I wouldn't expect nothing less from him, like Von is legit and cool as fuck, that's my man," Stasi said. I noticed Kaylen didn't say anything. I wasn't going to say anything because maybe I was overthinking the situation. That shit was kind of suspect because she always had some shit to say. *I wonder if she's fucking him or used to fuck him or what if she has a crush on him* I thought. I really liked Kaylen, but I would have to fuck her up if she thought she was going to take my man from me.

Stasi yelled, "What the fuck are we waiting on, I'm ready to blow this money, we got my homie's black card–shit, shopping spree on Von." Stasi started to walk, but stopped. "Ok girls, I'm not trying to alarm you, but I want to check and make sure that you both are strapped. I don't know why, but I have a very bad feeling that something isn't right," she asked me and Kaylen.

"Well I'm strapped and ready to blow a motherfucker's head off," Kaylen said as she patted her bag.

*

"So y'all don't think we're in danger?" Stasi asked; she had to make sure she was aware of her surroundings, because anything could happen. We decided to go ahead and go to Victoria's Secret and get some things.

"Do y'all see those four boys? They've been following us since we left the food court," I asked.

"Yes I saw them, I thought maybe they were intrigued by the Spanish, Haitian, and Jamaican chick," Kaylen admitted.

"I don't know what they doing, but I don't think it's that they; look crazy as fuck, for real," Stasi said. We finished up our shopping and decided to head to H&M and see what we could find our boos.

"Ok they done split up, what the fuck is really going on y'all?" I asked, now scared.

"Calm down, you know me and Kaylen strapped; if they try anything, we ready," Stasi told me. I didn't know what to do; I had never been in this type of situation before. I was actually scared and ready to go. I wasn't about shooting anybody or anybody getting hurt.

"Ok ladies, I'm about to get ready to go, I'm tired and those dudes are creeping me out, I can't take it anymore," I announced.

"Girl, if you don't suck that shit up put on your big girl panties and shop; fuck them dudes, I'm not leaving," Stasi snapped. I just walked off and headed towards the parking lot to my truck; they could be billy bad asses all they wanted, but I wasn't with that not one bit. I loved my life too damn much. I was looking down not paying attention as she started digging for her keys.

ZAT ZAT ZATTTTTTTTTTTTTTTTTTT….

“OMG, what the fuck was that!” I screamed as the only thing that registered was to dive to the ground. Somebody was shooting at me, and I didn't know what to do. I knew I couldn't run, because they could see me. “OMG OMG, I'm going to die,” I started crying. I had to muffle my sobs or they would find me for sure. Why didn't I listen and stay with Kay and Stasi?

“Aye, do you see the bitch? I hope we ain't hit her,” I heard someone yelling.

“Man no, I don't see her fuck, Chris is going to be pissed we didn't get her. I told you shooting at her wasn't a good idea, fool,” I heard another voice yelling. I started hearing police sirens as they got closer and closer; I was thankful they didn't hit me, because I definitely could’ve died.

“Fuck, let’s go, the police coming!” they yelled.

“MARISSAAAAA, oh my God girl, where are you!” Stasi yelled. I waited to get up to make sure those guys were gone; it was no telling if they were still hiding out.

KAYLEN

I was beyond pissed that Javon was talking to someone else. I thought he was playing a trick on me when he texted me that bullshit the other day. Now I see why this nigga ain't been returning my calls, because he with her ass. *It's plenty of nigga's that want me why the fuck did I cut off all my niggas for a hoe?* I thought. I chuckled because here I was a down ass chick and Javon picks a crybaby and a bitch green to the game.

I don't know what Marissa got going on, but this shit is crazy, like damn, you got dudes bussing guns at you in the mall parking lot in broad daylight? I guess I may as well keep it G with her though, because no matter how much I hate that her and Javon doing whatever, I'm not that type of friend to just hold back what's been going on with me and him, I thought to myself.

"OMG Marissa Marissaaaaa, where are you, are you ok?" I yelled. Me and Stasi walked around Marissa's car and saw her curled up behind the car.

"What is going on baby, why is this happening to you?" I questioned.

"Girl, Chris dumb ass put a hit out on me and Javon because I'm fucking with Javon now," Marissa cried.

"This boy is mad because you manned up and picked a real nigga versus his lame ass?" I screamed. I was blown; she couldn't be serious.

"That's pitiful as fuck. I've lost the teeny bit of respect I had left for him," Stasi explained.

"Come on girl, leave your truck here, let's hop in my truck and find Javon and let him know this shit can't be tolerated!" I yelled. I low key only said that because I think he forgot that me and her were friends, and this shit wasn't cool at all.

Lucky for them, I had just had my Range Rover cleaned yesterday. Not only was I Stasi's assistant, I was also a paralegal and I would soon be opening my very own business. I had just turned 25, I had my own condo at the Palazzo on St. Johns, and I loved it. Stasi, being the awesome boss she was, bought me a Range Rover as a sign on bonus. Stasi made sure it was my favorite color, lavender, and it was also customized. She also made sure that she upgraded it twice over the past 5 years I'd worked for her. We pulled up to Javon's house and walked towards the door.

DING DONG DING DONG! Marissa rung the doorbell.

"Oh hey, what's up ladies, come on in," Javon answered.

"Javon, we came to tell you the bullshit that just happened to her," I cautioned him. Javon tried to hide the look of surprise on his face when he noticed me there.

The shit I found funny was this massive ass house was nothing like the little ass apartment he'd been taking me to and had me pick furniture for.

"Ok I'm listening, what's wrong? What the hell happened to her?" he questioned.

"Well, we were in the avenues and some dudes kept following us; we told her to chill because we were strapped, but she left us and walked to her car, and someone started shooting at her," I explained. What I really wanted to say was she got spooked like a little bitch and ran, then the boys followed her and almost blew her fucking head off, but I'm not that mean–well, at least not right now.

JAVON

"What the fuck did you just say!" I screamed, "Did you just say those motherfuckers were shooting at my girl?" I questioned Kaylen.

"You fucking heard me Javon, don't act deaf now motherfucker," Kaylen snarled. One thing I didn't understand was why the fuck was Kaylen at my house with my girl. The second thing was why this bitch was yelling; she was definitely making it look like we fucked our something–damn man I thought to myself.

"Baby I'm so sorry, that punk is doing this because you're with me, but he's going to pay, I promise you that," I promised Marissa. "Y'all chill out, I'm about to call my people, this shit ain't gon' slide," I told them as I walked out of the room for a little privacy.

RING RING RING!

"Yo Yo, what up, boss man?" Marcus answered.

"Marcus, call Casey on three way ASAP, it's fucking urgent man," I demanded.

"Iight, hold on a minute B."

CLICK. RING

"Yo, what's the play, youngin," Casey answered.

"Can't call it OG, I got Jay on the other line, he said it's urgent," Marcus explained.

"10/4, let's see what's up, go ahead and add me in," Casey told him.

CLICK.

"Yo, everybody here?" Marcus asked.

"Here, I'm here," I said.

“I'm here,” Casey said.

“Alright so here's the problem, the dumb boy Chris feels like he can send his young bulls after my girl while she's in the mall; that shit ain't cool!” I yelled. I was beyond furious; I just got the woman I've always wanted, and her ex wants to start some war over it.

“The nigga did what, man? You can't be serious; he's taking his beef to your girl, like the nigga that pressed, yo?” Casey asked.

“I been noticed he was a fuck boy, nigga been hating on y’all since forever, and now he think he got a legit reason,” Marcus announced.

“But it can't even be that serious, like over a chick, really? You can't be that pressed for no pussy, bruh,” Casey stated.

“I don't give a fuck what he thought he had, or what he pressed about, it's millions of reasons why imma gut that nigga and leave his body pieces everywhere, and feed his guts to zoo animals,” I snarled. “Aye but check it, Imma kick it with my girl, calm her down, and then Imma hook up with y’all tomorrow so we can come up with a planned, BET?” I questioned.

“BET,” Casey and Marcus said in unison. I hung up from the call and decided to go talk to the girls, and advise them of what was going to happen.

“Alright, so peep this, Rissa is gonna kick it here with me for the night. I'll have somebody get her car and bring it here, and we're going to handle that nigga Chris ASAP. I can't continue to sleep on that nigga,” I advised them.

“Well alright, we out; you call us if you need us, Marissa. I don't care what time it is, just call us, we're here for you, love,” Kaylen advised. Stasi and Kaylen walked to the garage to get into Kaylen's truck and head back to Stasi's car.

"Baby I promise you, I'm so sorry; that nigga is going to pay, I promise, and I will make sure you are there to witness it," I expressed. *She just didn't know how serious I was about this my girl wasn't going to be scared to go anywhere because of him,* I thought. With the way Marissa was looking at me, I just felt like it wouldn't be right if I didn't protect her.

"Baby, I just want you to hold me right now, I have never in my life been this scared, just hold me daddy," she whispered. I swear after, she said that my, dick was on solid; if I got any harder, my pants and my dick would burst. I picked her up with a swoop and carried her all the way upstairs to my bedroom. I laid her on the bed and began to undress her slowly, never taking my eyes off her.

"I just want you to lay still and let me do everything, baby," I whispered. I undressed fully, then walked to the bathtub and filled it up with water and bubbles. I then ran to my mini fridge for some red wine. Looking back at Marissa she hadn't moved not one bit, I knew she was wondering what I was doing. Before she knew it, I was picking her up and placing her in the tub. I tied her hair up in a messy bun and handed her a glass of wine before stepping in the tub.

"Now if I do anything that you are uncomfortable with, just say the word and I will stop. I don't want to make you uncomfortable at all, ok?" I told her.

"We're grown Von, and anything that happens believe me, I'm ready," she said as she put her glass down and straddled me.

"Ohhhhhhh gawd, it's so big," she moaned as she started to ride me.

"Oh fuck, this pussy so tight," I moaned as I lifted her up and slammed her down. Water was splashing everywhere and we were fucking like none other. To say this was the best sex I'd ever had, was way beyond anything. Our chemistry was undeniable; it felt like our bodies were in sync. *Yeah she is definitely the one, I can't deny the Sparks that flew the whole time we made love* I thought. I didn't want to call it sex because I felt sex was something that was unheard.

JANEIRO

"Mmmm jis tank ou sa bitch (just like that, bitch)," I mumbled. After all these years, I never ever had sex with another woman. I only let a few bitches suck my dick.

"Ou so use dick a pi Bon (you suck the best dick)," I moaned as I pulled her hair. "Arghhhhhhhh," I moaned as I exploded in her mouth; the thing I loved was this bitch literally sucked every last drop out of me. When she realized she got all the nut from me, she stood up and went to the bathroom to fix herself up before she left. I grabbed my glass of Hennessy and walked towards my balcony. I decided that it was finally time that Stasi learned who "THE SPY" really was.

Ashley Jiménz walked from out of the bathroom. She was the only girl in her family that I allowed this close to me. She had been sent back and forth from Colombia to Haiti to pleasure me so that her family wouldn't be cut off; however, I figured she was growing tired of doing it for them.

"Alright Janeiro, I'm done cleaning up, you want to call José in to go ahead and search me so I can get out of here and make it back home?" she questioned.

"I don't need to search you. I have enough cameras everywhere to be able to tell if something was taken when I wasn't looking. I have already had the money wired to your account, and I would like to tell you your services are no longer needed. I know this is not something you want to do, and I will not continue to make you uncomfortable in any way, shape, or form," I explained.

“Thank you so much, you just don't know how much this means to me,” she said as she hugged me tight. “Thank you, and I wish you the best.” I waited until I saw her getting into her car from my monitors.

“José, come here please!” I yelled.

“Yes sir, what can I do to help?” José asked as he walked into the room.

“I would like for you to tell the spy it is time to make his presence known, and let her know exactly who he is,” I announced.

“Yes sir, I will definitely go ahead and do that, anything else?” José questioned.

“No that is all, now make it quick; he needs to be out of here very soon,” I explained.

*

I couldn't help but start to think of what Stasi was going to do when she found out that I was allowing the Jiménz family member Ashley to please me orally. She had been doing it for years, and I would just pay them or get rid of their debt, but I was tired of doing that; it seemed as if they decided to slack more and more. I knew that once she got back and explained that she had been dismissed, they were going to let it all out at the emergency meeting we had coming up tomorrow.

“Fuck Jiménz why didn't I think? Fuck, oh well. I'm a grown ass man. I never fucked her, just her mouth,” I chuckled. “They can't be mad at me because I got a little head,” I said.

I walked back and forth on the balcony, just thinking of how life would've been if my wife Talia was still alive. I never wanted to live this life; it was my wife's dream as a queen pin. I just took over because she died and she didn't want anyone that wasn't in our family taking over. I was attempting to fill my woman's shoes, but to be honest I didn't feel like I could fill them. I was only supposed to protect my wife, but somehow I failed awfully. I would never ever forget it, nor would I ever forgive myself.

LIEUTENANT DAVENPORT

I don't know what's going on? But I know she has something to do with that shooting on Moncrieff and Soutel. No matter how anybody tried to swing it, I thought to myself.

"Alright guys, listen up and listen closely!" I yelled. "We are attempting to get camera footage of what happened a few days ago at Winn-Dixie, where two men were killed and two drove off," I yelled. "We have some possible suspects," I continued as I turned and pointed towards the projection monitor. "First possible suspect is Casey D'Haiti, and he is considered armed and dangerous. The next possible suspect is Stasi Boudreaux; she is known here and in plenty of other states as the connect or queen pin. They are now seeing each other, so we think, well we hope, to find out everything; and whatever you find out, let me know. Alright, meeting is adjourned; don't contact me without any evidence that we can use to smash this bitch. Good luck," I yelled.

"Alright Julian, give me your view on this, what do you think?" I questioned my partner. I think you need to leave Ms Boudreaux out of it. You have no direct link that she is connected, and you are going to create a war that we cannot handle," he honestly told me.

I knew, Detective Julian Sands had no problem attempting to catch a criminal; however, he knew danger, and Stasi reeked of danger and death. I don't know why be he felt I only had a hard on for Stasi because of who her father was? To him that wasn't a good enough excuse. He is not in the country anymore nor will he step foot here and if he did he wasn't stupid enough to get caught.

"Look Julian, I want her so bad I can taste it; she thinks she's so legit, but I'm not fucking stupid!" I yelled as I slammed my hand on the desk.

"Derrick, you have to chill man, you are 35; you will give yourself a heart attack trying to do this, for real. It's serious, but not that serious," Sands told me.

CHRIS

"Thank you for tuning into Channel 4 news; coming up at 11 pm, we are going to take a look into a drive-by shooting that was done on Edgewood and Lem Turner."

I went ahead and muted the TV. I was happy that my boys did the damn thing. I decided to try and call my mother's phone again

"We're sorry, you have reached a number that is disconnected or is no longer in service; if you feel you have reached this recording in error, please check the number and try your call again."

" Man, what the fuck is going on?" I said as I threw my cellphone; this is some bullshit. I went by my mother's house earlier and was a little confused, because most of her clothes were gone, and the kids' car seats, along with some of their clothes and toys were gone. I just didn't understand, because her car was still there, so whoever they went with was the person driving. I heard knocking at the door and grabbed my glock 19 before I crept to the door. I opened the door and stood behind the door, and there were my boys rushing to get in.

"Man, if you don't move your paranoid ass out our way," Melvin demanded.

"Don't push me, fat boy!" I yelled as I pushed Melvin back. So tell me what the fuck happened, I saw something on the news, how many people were hit?" I asked. I was excited as fuck to hear about what went down.

"Man, it was a gang of them out there. I don't know how many we actually hit forreal; we just set if off and pulled off, no stopping no nothing, slow creep," Melvin explained.

"Well it's 10:58, so it's about to come on in a second," I announced while looking at my watch.

"*Thank you for staying tuned in for the 11 o clock news, we now have Sarah Garrett coming live from the scene. Yes this is Sarah Garrett, and I'm down at the scene of an apparent drive-by shooting that has injured 9 men and 2 children, and killed 2 people. We're not sure of the status of the victims of this time. The deceased victims and the children shot were not actually outside, but in the apartment building behind where the men were standing, and bullets went inside the apartment, injuring the children and killing the adult. We will have names of the other victims soon. If you have any information on this shooting, please call 1-800-CRIME-STOPPERS–back to you Tasha.*

"You idiots only killed 2 people, and one was by mistake? Who in the hell taught you dumbasses how to shoot," I uttered. This didn't make any bit of sense to me.

"Man, we injured 9 people and killed one for sure that was out there hanging; they didn't say the status of the other people, so there's no telling what they got going on. You need to chill the fuck out man," Melvin snapped.

"Fuck you man, your fucking kids and mother aren't missing, mine are. I can say whatever the fuck I want until they asses pop the fuck up!" I screamed. I tried to think of what else I could do that would make Jay come out of hiding, and also help me find my family.

THE SPY

I can't believe this is really about to happen, I thought as I boarded the plane. For the past 3 ½ years, I had been following Stasi around, making sure that there was no harm done to her. I didn't know how she would feel about me once she found out about me, but I was extremely excited. It kind of felt like my heart was about to beat out of my chest.

"We have a clear landing sir, so we will be landing in the next 5 minutes, so if you don't mind buckling up, please," the pilot spoke. *Great we're about to land*, I thought

ME: I made it, I'm about to check in the hotel, shower, and then call her

BOSS: She is already at the room

ME: oh wow, ok, well I'll be there shortly

BOSS: ok, keep me posted

I decided to go ahead and put on my seatbelt so we could land and I could change out of my clothes. I looked out the window and wondered why there were police cars and a SWAT team waiting. *What the fuck is going on*, I said to myself. I was actually glad I didn't grab my guns, because I definitely would've been screwed. I remained calm and waited to completely land before I got up out of my seat. We landed, so I proceeded to go ahead and get out of my seat, so I could head towards the jet's door to see what was going on. I stepped down the stairs, and as soon as one of the cops flashed their badge, I held my hand up.

“If you are not the person in charge, everything that is about to come out of mouth is highly irrelevant. I would love the person in charge, and very quickly,” I advised. I wasn't with the bullshit, and I wanted to make it brutally clear.

Lieutenant Davenport walked up and stated, I'm very sorry sir we were told this jet was landing from Haiti we were expecting someone else. We are very sorry about the inconvenience we hope you have a pleasant afternoon Lieutenant Davenport apologized as he started walking away. It's nothing to see here wrap it up and let's head out this was false call. What the fuck now that's some freaky shit whats going on why the hell where they here. I definitely have to make sure I mention this to Stasi. I hopped into the awaiting Tahoe even more ready to get to the hotel.

STASI

“Girl take me to the Hilton downtown for some reason my dad texted me saying I needed to stay there I told Kaylen. Alright we'll be there in about ten minutes' girl I'll pick you up tomorrow for work” Kaylen advised me. I still couldn't believe Marissa's ass was shot at. Like who the fuck would do some shit like that?

“Kay, don't forget that tomorrow I will be leaving to go to Haiti for two days to handle some personal affairs, so you of course are in charge,” I reminded Kaylen.

“Yes ma'am, I didn't forget, you know I got your back girl,” Kaylen joked. We pulled up to the hotel, and I got out to get checked in.

"Ah, to what do we owe the lovely pleasure, Ms. Boudreaux?" the receptionist asked.

"I'm here to check in for the night. I should already have a reservation," I advised him.

"Yes ma'am, you're in the penthouse; enjoy your stay, and thank you for returning to the Hilton," he smiled. I got on the elevator, and when I got to the penthouse, someone was already sitting on the couch.

"Alright, I'm sure my dad sent you, so to what do I owe the pleasure?" I quizzed the person. He stood up, and I swear I was staring at a spitting image of my father, except years younger.

"What the hell, who are you, and why are you here?" I grabbed my .38 out of my purse and aimed it at him.

"Chill out, Stasi. I'm your brother Stacey, and dad sent me here to let you know who I am, and why I'm here," he stuttered.

"You are not my brother, my brother died 21 years ago, right along with my mom," I cried.

"You can call dad if you don't believe me. I also have my birth certificate, my license, and passport in that bag," he pointed towards the bag. I told him to have a seat and called my father to make sure he wasn't lying to me.

RING RING RING

"Ki se pitit frè ou (that is your brother child)."

"Ki jan mwen te panse li mouri (how I thought he died)?" I asked.

"Mwen pral eksplike lè ou retounen ti bebe (I will explain when you return baby)" my father murmured.

I hung up the phone and looked at my little brother. I put down my gun, and ran and jumped in his arms as he stood up. I couldn't do anything but cry; here I was thinking that my brother was gone, and the entire time he was alive.

"Why did you guys hide you not dying from everyone for 21 damn years!" I yelled as I smacked him across the head.

"Well, Pops wanted to keep it quiet because his rival Black actually had, well probably still has, a hit out with anyone with our last name," he announced.

"Wow, that's fucked up to the tenth power, so what exactly do you do?" I asked; I had a million questions.

"Well as of right now, I'm your protector & your gunman when need it, your scheduler any time there is a shipment, and your assistant for messages or anything that needs to be relayed to you."

Well, my question is if you're alive, why haven't you been getting groomed for the business?"

"Well, this is actually a woman's business; the man watches and makes sure she is protected, and that no harm comes her way. So if you think that I'm jealous or bitter, no–I love doing my job as your little brother to make sure you're good at all times. The only problem you may have is Casey not wanting to stop doing business to be your protector," he told me.

What do you mean by that?" I asked, puzzled.

"Well, being that you have taken over completely, your boyfriend or husband is supposed to protect you at all times, so if you are what he wants, he has to rethink what he is doing, or leave you alone," he explained.

"Well we aren't dating yet, and I'm not sure if we will be. I'm not about to rush into anything with him just to have a protector," I told him.

We continued to sit and talk until the wee hours of the morning, until we both fell asleep.

CASEY

I wonder what Stasi got going on? I thought, as I looked at the clock it was 3 am. I decided it was way to early to call her and bother her,but that would be the first thing on my agenda when I woke up. I laid in bed and thought about what life with Stasi would be like. I really wanted to be with her; she was everything that I was looking for in a woman–smart, mean at times, thick as fuck, and it didn't hurt she busted her guns like one of us. I decided I might as well go ahead and drift off to sleep for a little while so I could be somewhat refreshed when I woke up.

*

"Casey, what you doing baby?" Stasi asked.

"Nothing babe, I'm about to run downstairs right quick, you want something?"

"No, just hurry back so you can put me to sleep," she smiled. I ran downstairs and looked at the mess that was down there.

*"What the...." **CLICK CLICK**...i heard a gun cock behind me; I couldn't believe I got caught slipping in my crib, basically naked . I just hoped that Stasi didn't come downstairs I didn't want anything to happen to her.*

"Look here whoever the fuck you are you got the wrong motherfucker to be coming in here trying to rob." "

Well I guess it's a good thing I'm not here to rob you dumb ass" The person said.

BOOM… *I felt a sharp pain in my head and everything went black.*

*

RING RING

I jumped up sweating.

"Man, what the fuck kind of dream was that? Sheesh." I checked my whole body before grabbing my cellphone.

"Talk to me."

"Aye Casey, a few people from our crew got hit off Edgewood and Lem Turner; we're heading over to Baptist downtown right now, where Javon's cousin Tej wife works, so she can give us all the info we need since we not related to none of them."

"Iight bet, I'll be there in 30 minutes." I grabbed some grey sweats, a white polo V-neck, and my wallet, then I put on my wolf grey foamposites. I went to the bathroom and brushed my teeth, and washed my face before heading downstairs.

I decided I was going to take my '98 Crown Victoria and head out. I made my way downtown, wondering if Chris really had the balls to do all this. I pulled into a parking spot at the hospital and headed towards the waiting area, where I saw everyone standing and waiting to find out what was going on.

"What's up fellas, what's the news?"

"Nobody has came and told us anything yet," Javon said.

"Alright, well how did this happen? Why weren't they paying attention?"

“We're not sure; we do know two kids got hit, and someone in their house died from bullets that went through the window,” Javon answered.

“That's fucked up; you already know that funeral is taken care of by us–that shouldn't have happened.”

*

“Hey y'all,” Teedra said as she walked out.

“What's up cuh,” Javon answered.

“What's up ma,” I acknowledged.

“Well, you had in total 11 people come in, including the kids. One of the kids was shot in the shoulder, and one was grazed in the ear,” she explained as she looked at the charts. “The 9 adults were hit in different areas–shoulder, hand, thigh, stomach, foot and back. None are life threatening, however, we are going to announce that everyone is dead except the kids, so they don't expect any retaliation from the ones shot, she warned.

“Alright, thanks cuh, we appreciate you giving us that info,” Javon expressed as he gave his cousin-in-law a hug.

“So how we gon’ handle this? I figure this was the idiot Chris thinking that if he shot us up, he would be stopping us, but he ain't know that was nothing.”

“I don't know, this nigga just shot at my girl a few days ago, and I'm not about to just let that shit go, we got handle it. Aye, you know what? Hit up Marcus and tell him to handle one of those kids. I don't give a fuck which one, but it needs to be done ASAP,” Javon demanded.

“I'll hit him up. I'm about to hit it, I want to catch Stasi before she heads to work.”

*

ME: Handle one of those problems

Marcus: Does it matter which one I do first?

ME: One of the pink ones, doesn't matter

Marcus: How soon?

ME: Yesterday

Marcus: 10/4, consider it handled

ME: Bet!

I walked out the hospital, headed towards the parking lot, and hopped in my Crown Vic. I decided to just pop up on Stasi since she hadn't called me or returned any of my calls. I drove to her house and walked to the front door.

DING DONGGGG..

Hello Mr. Casey, how are you today?” Rebecca, Stasi's maid, answered.

“I'm fine, is Stasi here?”

“No she isn't, she didn't come home last night, she told me she had a meeting and would not be home,” Rebecca advised.

“Iight thanks, have a good day, Rebecca.”

MARCUS

Fuck I do not want to do this, I thought. I decided that since everyone was still sleep, I would just go ahead and get it over with, so I could act like I was just waking up; luckily, everyone was in their own bedroom. I grabbed my silenced 9mm, and crept towards the rooms where the twins were sleeping. I couldn't decide which one to kill; honestly, I didn’t want to kill either but I had to, so I just picked a room and went in. I grabbed the pillow and repented, although I knew I was still going to hell for killing this innocent child. I pulled the trigger three times and walked out the room. I hurried downstairs, wrapped a towel over my hand, busted the window, and then opened the door to make it look as if someone came in. I ran to my room, changed my shirt, and washed my hands with bleach and soap, then proceeded out of my room as if i had just woke up. I heard Ms. Williams scream, so I ran towards the twin’s room.

“OMG OMG, I thought we were safe, arghhhhhhhhhh, look at my grand baby, look at what they did to her, nooooo, oh God no,” she whimpered as she held her.

“What the fuck! How did this happen!” I yelled, as if I didn't know what had transpired.

“You got to do something, you got to do something,” she cried as she rocked her back and forth.

“Let me call our cleaning crew; they are the only ones that are able to get into the morgue with no issues.”

*

"Where is her phone and the iPad she had?" I asked.

"They are right here, it looks like she was texting someone; she even told them the address, could it have been them?" she questioned. I was actually really surprised; I didn't even think to check her phone, because I didn't expect her to be texting anyone.

"Fuck! What the fuck, you weren't checking their phones?" I screamed.

"I didn't check them last night, I forgot. I should have. OMG, my baby, my baby," she cried. Fuck, I had to text Von. I didn't know who she was texting, but we definitely had to find out, and quick–we could be in danger.

ME: She was texting someone, check the number (904) 213-0978

Von: what did she say!

ME: She sent the address, we about to haul ass, can't take no chances

Von: no doubt, keep me posted

ME: Fasho!

"Ok, we have to get out of here, and quick; my crew is on the way. We cannot continue to sit here; we are basically sitting ducks right now, being as we don't know who did this."

"Let me just grab our stuff," Ms. Williams said.

While gathering my stuff, I tried to think of who she could have been texting. I grabbed all of my things, and then wiped everything down, although i knew the crew was going to do it; I just had to make sure I covered my tracks. We hurried to my rental truck and threw everything in; just as we were backing up, the cleaning crew was coming up.

"Handle that for me, and you know we got y'all. Do a full wipe down; keys are on the kitchen counter."

I decided that we would stay at the Hilton Regency in Savannah until we could get a house that was free for us to stay at.

*

ME: 2 W Bay St is where we are for now

Von: bet money will be on the room within the hour

ME: bet we need a secluded house ASAP

Von: already on it I'll hit you later

ME: 10/4

I was still actually hurt. I had to kill Carlee and all because of her dad and his stupidity. This was the first kill I had ever done that made me sick to my stomach and my heart was hurting. Chris Jr. was too young to understand but Carleigh was distraught over losing her twin sister. I had to walk away before I told on myself; this was going to be hard because I felt so bad.

"Ms. Williams I have to make a few runs–don't open the door unless you order room service. Don't make any calls and I will be back shortly. I'm going to tell Chris what happened. I don't know if he's being watched, so I don't want to speak over the phone."

"Ok baby, please be careful, and I promise we won't make anymore mistakes. I can't lose another one of my babies," she cried. I walked out and headed towards my truck to find out what was going on.

MARISSA

I went over the last couple of days in my head, and I was still astonished that Chris would set up a hit on me. I felt that with all the drama I went through trying to be with him through everything, that he would never bring me any harm, but boy was I wrong. I knew that he thought I was stupid, and didn't know that he was just using me to try and get in with Stasi. At first Chris hated Stasi's guts, but then when he heard rumors about who she could be, all of a sudden that was his girl. I couldn't help but shake my head. This man had 3 kids on me. I swear, I just wanted to blow his brains out, and then I wanted to blow his mama's brains out for lying right along with him, but I had to remember that Chris was Ms. William's son, and she had no obligation to me at all.

*

I wondered what was going on with Javon and his crew; he got a call and jumped up, then ran out the house. I prayed it had nothing to do with the shooting on Edgewood and Lem Turner. I was just ready for this shit to be all over. As I thought about it, I realized I wasn't exactly ready for this lifestyle, not one bit. I swear, I tried to act tough, but truth was I wasn't as tough as Stasi, and I swear I hated it.

I got out of the bed and decided to go ahead and get my stuff together so that i could leave Javon's house. I didn't want to become too dependent on him, and I wasn't ready for this. While cleaning out my side of the closet I didn't hear Javon come up.

"Where you think you going?" he asked. I turned around.

"I didn't think you would make it back before I was gone, but this isn't the life for me. Chris was never this huge to have bounties placed on my head and shit. I just want to be with somebody that doesn't care about this drug shit and is official. I don't want to go to jail behind the man I love, and be stuck because what the fuck am I supposed to do–lie or tell the truth? I don't want to hurt you, or anybody for that matter, so I think it's best that I leave and let Chris know I'm not with you, so this can be squashed." He moved towards me and grabbed my face and looked in my eyes.

"Baby, when I tell you this shit is over for me, I mean it; the only reason why I'm out in the streets making moves is because this boy attempted to cause harm to my future wife. I don't give a fuck about any money left out in these streets. I'm a fucking billionaire 10 times over, so nothing is keeping me in the streets besides killing that bastard so that my woman can be at peace. Now if you were to leave me because of him, then this city would be painted crimson red, and his body parts would be every fucking where until I got you back, so the choice is yours," Javon told her as he walked out the room.

*

Fuck that I'm not about to give anybody the satisfaction of seeing me look weak. My man loves me and I know he will handle Chris's punk ass and soon. I decided to hop in the shower and try to make it to see Stasi's jet take-off I just wanted or more so needed my best friend's opinion even though I knew what she was going to say. I finished showering and decided to slip into something quick. I slipped into a Victoria secret short set and some Michael Kors sneakers grabbed my phone, my keys, shades and black card and proceeded downstairs. I saw that Javon was having a meeting with some of his boys but i knew i needed to tell him I was heading out. Hey baby I'm about to try and catch Stasi before she heads out of town i advised him. Mm, you looking damn good baby," he eyed me up and down he loved when i wore my hair down. She just looked good enough to eat and he was a little hungry.

"Alright ma, I'm sending two of my young bulls behind you so that they can keep an eye on you. You won't be caught by yourself anymore, I promise," he advised. He gave me a kiss and snapped his fingers so the two ruthless cats could follow behind me. Anything happens to her it happens to your family understand motherfuckers he warned. Yes sir we understand they murmured.

CHRIS

I was so tired of trying to think of where my mother and kids could be.

RING RING RING….

"What's up, Lauren?"

"Something is wrong, Chris, something is really really wrong," Lauren cried.

"What do you mean, is somebody there? What you mean something is wrong?"

"Nobody is here. I'm not trying to set you up, Chris; something is going on. Something has happened to one of the girls, or maybe both. All of a sudden, I'm feeling sick to the pit of my stomach," she sniffled.

"I don't understand, how do you just think this? You sure you not sick, man? What you ate? It could be food poisoning."

"It's not fucking food poisoning Chris, it's mother's intuition. Anytime one of my babies is sad, happy, hurt, or whatever, I can feel it. I'm their mother, I carried them for 8 ½ months, not you!" she yelled. I knew I was pissing her off, but I wanted to make sure she wasn't just tripping, because sometimes she overreacted.

*

"Look, I'm going to check into it, ma. I just want you to chill and I'll be there within the next 20 minutes; just try and stay calm for me." I hoped that nothing was wrong with my kids, because I didn't know how long I would be able to control myself. As I hung up with Lauren, I got a few text messages.

904-213-0978: Hi Mr. Williams I am Carlee's classmate. I don't know what's going on, but last night Carlee texted me asking me to text this number and say that she felt something was wrong.

ME: Who is this

904-213-0978: I'm just her classmate sir. I don't want any problems. I just did what she asked me to do

ME: Have you talked to her today?

904-213-0978: no sir, the number is disconnected now

ME: if you hear anything, please don't hesitate to text or call

904-213-0978: yes sir I will, I promise

ME: thank you

*

I decided to check the other messages I had. I also was still trying to figure out what the fuck was going on.

*

UNKNOWN: How well do you take care of your kids?

ME: What the fuck you mean?

UNKNOWN: You can't protect your family, that's all I'm saying

ME: Fuck you, I can protect my family

UNKNOWN: We'll see soon enough

*

I didn't know what the fuck was going on now, but I absolutely needed to find out. If someone hurt my family, I promise I wouldn't sleep until everyone was dead. I now felt stupid, because no one should've been able to touch my family; they should've been far away from the hood as possible. I decided to hurry up and make my way towards Lauren's house to see if she still felt the same way about the kids being hurt I hopped into my Impala, not thinking that it wasn't one of my bulletproof cars. I was driving down 103rd and I could've sworn I saw Miles. I know this fuck nigga ain't just driving around all willy nilly, like I don't have him doing something. I decided fuck it, let's see, so I made an illegal U-turn and decided to follow the truck. I wanted to see if it was really Miles. I followed the truck until it came to a stop at the Raceway on Cassatt Ave. I watched the person get out, and low and behold, it was Miles.

"What's up nigga, you ain't been returning my calls, what's up with that?"

"Man I been out here day and night searching for your mom and kids, but what you not about to do is treat me like I'm your fucking do boy," Marcus yelled.

"You gon' do whatever the fuck I tell you to do, my nigga; you the one out here working for me."

"I was trying to be civil and understanding because your family is missing, but fuck you, I don't have to put up this shit!" Marcus yelled. I was so upset I pulled my gun out and stuck it in Marcus' side.

"Say something else nigga, and I'll blow you away; your ass is going to help, or you're going to die just like your crew."

"If you going to pull a gun, you better use it because I'm not going to be so nice. I can assure you I'm the fucking killer, not you," Marcus snarled. Marcus yanked away from me and hopped in his rental. I didn't think about what I had done until Marcus was long gone. *Fuck, what the hell did I do? He's going to fucking kill me*. I hopped in my car and headed towards Lauren's house; I had to get her away and fast.

KAYLEN

I was trying so damn hard to not text Javon and bother him, but I just couldn't believe he texted me and told me it was over.

"Does he not know who the fuck I am?" I screamed. I was literally drunk, and it wasn't even 11 am yet. I put so much into trying to get Javon, and then Marissa just breaks up with Chris and sees Javon, and she just gets him like that.

"Fuck that! He's my man! He's my man!" I yelled as I threw my Patrón bottle at the wall. My hair was a mess, and so was my condo and as soon as I dropped Stasi off last night, I came straight home to drink and mope. I was going to get my man back; Marissa wasn't shit but a Spanish crybaby bitch that had nothing on my Jamaican accent, my big natural ass, and my breasts. I was going to get up and head to do my hair, then drive by his house and see what he said.

"He can't resist me at all," I said out loud. I grabbed a YSL short tracksuit and my Louboutin sneakers. I was about to hop in the shower; I couldn't let anyone see me tore up. I would not ruin my reputation.

*

I hopped out of the shower looking and feeling like a new person. I decided on no bra since my breasts didn't sag. I put on some lace boy shorts, and then put my clothes on. I slipped on my shoes, took my phone off the charger, and grabbed my car keys, feeling sexy as hell. I got in my Range Rover and headed to the apartment where he took his "bitches" no one had the pleasure of having sex with him in his bed at his mini-mansion, but Marissa. I also wondered why I never got to go to his house; I always thought the apartment was where he laid his head.

I pulled up to the apartment and got out, and as I was walking in, the doorman stopped me.

"If you're going to visit Mr. Burns, he moved out I'd say about two to three days ago," he informed me.

"Oh yeah, I forgot he did tell me he moved. I really forgot; thanks for reminding me," I answered. I turned around and walked back to my Range.

I was literally pissed off; this man had really tried me like I was some slut. What i wasn't going to do was let him get away with playing me like this hell no I couldn't. I decided it was time to roll up on him and his boys. I knew nine times out of ten, they were at his cousin Tej's auto shop, so I headed that way.

*

I pulled up to Tej's auto shop and got out and walked inside. i had seen everyone's car out front so I knew he was there

"Yes, can you tell Jay to come to the front, please?" I asked the receptionist.

"Sure, give me one moment, the receptionist advised me as she got up to go to the back. "You have somebody in the front asking for you to come up there, Jay," the receptionist told him.

"Yo, what you doing here, Kay? I told you I couldn't fuck with you no more because I'm with Rissa," he explained to.

"Yeah, I know what you TEXTED me, but you ain't tell me you treating me like some slut bitch," I snarled.

"It's not even like that Kay, you know I fuck with you baby, it's just I've been trying to fuck with Marissa for years. I swear, I'm not trying to hurt you Kay, but you gotta understand me," he expressed.

"I understand, but that's not the way to go about it; if you feeling somebody else, you let me know up front, don't send me no fuck ass text, that's not cool!" I yelled as I turned around and left before I started crying; his hoe ass wasn't nowhere worth my tears.

JAVON

What the fuck just happened I thought to myself. I didn't want that shit to go down like that; Kay was my girl, like I loved the fuck out her and she was extremely cool, and she rode for a nigga with no questions asked, but I was just intrigued with Marissa at this time.

"I got to make it up to her, I can't let it go down like this, I can't," I said out loud. I went back to my boys to let them know I was about to leave.

"Alright y'all boys, I'm about to hit it, I got a little issue I have to handle," I said.

"Ok, but don't forget that the cleaning crew got one of Chris' daughters, and we need to let them know what we want to do with her ASAP," one of the members of the crew announced.

"Yeah I know, and tell them to go ahead and chop her up; have the grandma call the news and report her missing tomorrow, Marcus, and then the next day, I want Chris to wake up with her head in a box on his front porch. I want her mom to walk to her car and find a arm, and the news station to change shifts and find a leg–that motherfucker is going to learn not to fuck with us," I demanded.

"He pulled a gun on me, so he better hope I don't see him before then, because I'm shooting first and asking questions later–that's that," Marcus stated.

*

I left from my cousin's shop and headed towards Kaylen's condo. I prayed she was there; I really felt bad. I actually didn't realize I had sent the text to Kaylen; that's what I get for rushing. I finally pulled up to Kaylen's condo and saw her Range Rover out front.

"Great, I can talk to her," I said out loud. I parked, then proceeded towards the building. I decided to take the stairs so she would be surprised. As soon as I got off the elevator and knocked on the door, Kaylen answered in nothing but a bra and panty set, with her robe open.

"Mi don't understand why yu no use the elevator bwoy," she declared.

"I didn't use the elevator because I wanted to surprise you when I came up," I uttered.

"Mi no give a damn that yu here, dirty bwoy," she pointed out.

"That may be the case, but I came to let you know I didn't mean to hurt you. I just don't know what to do," I confessed.

"Mi don't know wah yu here, mon," she ranted. I had to look down; she looked so good just standing there in barely nothing, and my dick was hard as hell.

"I just don't want things to end ugly with us; you were my friend before anything. I don't want to lose that," I pleaded as I grabbed her hand.

"Mi naa bout fi ramp wit yu bwoy (I'm not about to play with you boy)," she claimed. Truth be told, she knew I was going to come by that's why she rushed home to shower and change. She also set up her security system to record everything. Payback was a bitch.

I pulled her onto my lap, and I just couldn't keep my hands off her. She was nothing like Marissa, and that's what I loved about her; her accent also helped–it turned me on BAD. I started kissing her, and as soon as I started to take off her robe…

RING RING RING....

I shook my head and grabbed my phone. I looked at it, and it was Marissa calling. I didn't have the heart to answer, so I let it ring out.

"Look, I got to go. I'll be back, ok?" I pleaded as I kissed her and walked out the door.

*

What the fuck was I about to do in there, I asked myself when I got into my car. I'm with Marissa I can't be fooling around with Kaylen like that anymore,man, I thought. I drove off with no destination in mind. I just needed to hurry up and get away from Kaylen's house before I did something I shouldn't. I found himself at the club and decided to see how they had done the past few nights, since I hadn't had a chance to make it in. I promise, once Chris was 6 feet deep, I would be in my club every night seeing how everything was going.

"What's up Shanice, how have we been doing the past couple of nights?" I asked.

We've done really good Jay, all the numbers are on your desk in your office; if you need me, just let me know," she informed me. I proceeded to the office and sat down so I could go over the numbers. Damn, we did damn good Wednesday night; looks like all the heavy hittas were here–we made $500,000. I looked, and all 20 of the V.I.P areas were purchased, and everyone had bought expensive bottles; I was ecstatic. I turned around to check the monitors, and noticed there were 8 men in ski masks with guns walking around the club.

"What the fu–"

"Hands up, big money," I heard someone say.

"I'm not putting my fucking hands up, so if you gon' shoot me then shoot me, and let that be it," I snarled. I wasn't the type to bow down. I grabbed my glass of Patrón and took a sip; I wasn't scared to die, and I think that's what scared the gunman.

"Where's the money at, money man?" the gunman asked. I laughed as I took another sip of my Patrón.

"You come in my establishment asking me where the fuck my money is, and think I'm going to give it to you?" I laughed. "You got me fucked up. Good luck fuck boy, but guess what? Lights out," I said. The gunmen looked behind him too late; he was hit in the head by Marcus with a bat.

"Good looking my boy, I wasn't gon' let that nigga get nothing though, but you showed up just in time," I confessed. "I would've been a dead motherfucker if you hadn't showed up."

"We duct-taped the gunman, and went downstairs to make sure everyone was ok.

"We're going to be closed for tonight so we can get this taken care of, because someone done tried the wrong motherfucker. I don't think they know exactly who they fucking with, but believe me, I'm going to fucking show them."

STASI

I was tired as hell, but I wasn't going to let my dad nor my brother know that. Man, I can't believe I can say I have a brother. I was still shocked, but I was happy as hell. I, now had a sibling to talk to.

"Alright lil brother, let's get off this jet and head to dad's so we can get ready for this meeting," I insisted. We both unbuckled our seat belts and headed towards the door of the jet. Once we were off, we headed towards our driver and the rented Suburban truck. We were surprised when we got in.

"Well Ms. Boudreaux, we meet again. I come in peace for now," the head of the Jiménz family quipped.

"Whether you were here in peace or not doesn't fucking matter, but right now you are out of line being in my truck, and I have every right to blow your fucking brains out," I cautioned.

"I'm coming to tell you that your father is a piece of shit, and I have proof," he snarled.

"Your proof better be damn good, because you're making me late," I warned.

"Your father has been having my daughter suck his dick for the past 5 years, and he gave us the money to pay of our debt to you; he recently cut her off on her last visit," he emphasized. I didn't say anything. I didn't know whether to believe him; this could be a distraction to knock me off my square.

"Stacey, call Josè and let him know that we are going to be a little late because we are having car issues. Driver, if anyone calls, we are having car issues; lift up the hood and act like you are taking a peek."

"Yes ma'am, I will do that now," the driver said as he took off his hat and blazer.

*

"Now what proof do you have, Mr. Jiménz? You meet us in our truck accusing my father of allowing your daughter to suck his dick for well over 5 years, but you're just now saying something because he cut her off? Do you know how that makes you look?" I questioned him. "It makes you look like a bitter motherfucker. You need to come up with this proof, and I mean that or you already know the consequences."

"I have the proof coming right up. I'm waiting for Ashley to text me the pictures she snuck," he told me.

"Hey José, I need you to let everyone know that we are going to be a little late, we are having some car troubles," my brother told José. "Tell my dad not to worry, we will be there…wait, what did you just say? You said Ashley is there to make an announcement? Ok ummm, tell her to please wait patiently, we will be there shortly," he said as he hung up.

"What? What did you just say?" Mr. Jiménz asked.

"He said that YOUR daughter Ashley is at the meeting waiting on us to give an announcement," I reiterated.

"Fuck, why would she do that!" Mr. Jiménz hopped out of the truck and ran to his waiting town car, and sped off.

"Driver, let's go, we need to head to our fathers place, NOW," I demanded. The driver hopped in the car and sped off quick; within 10 minutes, we were pulling inside the gate of my father's mansion.

*

Me and my brother walked into my father's house, and everyone was mingling drinking wine.

"Afternoon lady and gentlemen. I am sorry we are late; we ran into someone stating that he wanted to let me know that my father was a lying piece of shit," I said as I glared at my dad. He didn't acknowledge me, nor did he turn around from talking on his phone.

"Well if you all don't mind, I am ready to head to the sub-level basement for this meeting to begin." I grabbed my glass and bottle of Patrón, and led the way to the sub-basement, where meetings were held. I sat down as I waited for the heads of the families, as well as my father and Ashley to have a seat; once everyone was seated, I began.

"Ok, the main reason why I wanted to hold this meeting was because I received the numbers from the middle of the month, and not all of them were good. Rasmussen, Lè'Roux, and Patel families– you all have already made the full payment we were requesting from you in two weeks, and we are extremely grateful for that, so when you are ready to re-up, we will give you 100 keys free–no payment needed. If you have any concerns, please let me know now," I said as I looked around.

"Actually, I do have an issue I need to discuss," the Rasmussen family head raised his hand.

"Yes Mr. Rasmussen, what is the issue?" I asked.

"Well, I am not a 100% sure, but a few of my workers, who are connected with the Jiménz crew, were told that Mr. Jiménz wanted to kill you and your father and take over," he sighed.

"Thank you very much for the information, Mr. Rasmussen; you three may go ahead and leave." This shit was getting very crazy, and I wasn't with it. As they left, I looked to the remaining two family heads and Ashley.

"So Ashley, what was the announcement you wanted to make?" I asked. Ashley stood up.

"Well, I just wanted you to know that whatever my father told you was a lie. I never in my life did anything with your father. He also was planning on killing you when you got into your truck earlier, but he," she pointed to my brother, "was there and interrupted his plan." I was; livid this bitch thought he could successfully kill me without a big problem?

"Mr. Arpasi, your problem is nowhere as big as this issue; consider this a warning. You are dismissed," I said as I shooed him out.

CONFIDENTIAL INFORMANT

DETECTIVE SANDS

I wasn't about to let Davenport get me killed; he wasn't thinking with his head honestly. I was nervous to do this, because I could lose my badge, but I would rather lose my badge than my life. I pulled my hoodie over my face and walked towards the back of the club. I didn't know how Javon Burns would take me coming into his club unannounced. I walked upstairs to where I thought his office should be and knocked.

KNOCK…KNOCK…KNOCK…

"Come in," I heard Javon say. I entered and before I could walk in fully, I was snatched from behind. Javon had this big ass security guard holding me by my neck, while he searched me for guns. Lucky for me, I decided it wouldn't be a good idea for me to take anything inside with me.

"Detective Sands, I would say to what do I owe the pleasure, but I don't fuck with cops, so why the fuck are you here?"

"I just wanted to make you and Casey aware of my partner's plan," I said.

"Well what is the plan? You're not telling me shit, and you're pissing me off," Javon said.

"Ok I'm sorry, so I don't know if you guys know about the Edgewood and Lem Turner shooting, but my partner is trying to pin it on Casey and Stasi."

"What the fuck, you can't be serious, they didn't have anything to do with that," Javon yelled.

“That I am pretty sure of, but my partner is trying to get the video surveillance from all the stores surrounding the area, so if I was anybody in that situation, I would handle those tapes before I don't know, maybe tomorrow around 5,” I said.

“Alright bet, well look, take this phone.” Javon handed me an iPhone 6.

“The code is 0918; if you enter it 8190, the entire phone erases and it appears as a regular phone. What I want you to do is record anything that may lead us to his next move.”

“I can do that as long as you remember to keep me off the hit list if and when the time comes,” I said.

“Deal,” Javon said as he stood and shook my hand. “Now hurry up and get out of here before someone sees you,” he said.

“Alright I'm out, if there is anything else I can do, let me know,” I said as I put the iPhone in my pocket, pulled my hoodie back on my head, and disappeared into the shadows.

JANEIRO

I didn't know why the fuck Ashley just lied, but thank goodness she did; my daughter would've been pissed, but what I couldn't understand was why Mr. Jiménz thought he was going to kill my daughter because he was cut off. I was facing the window collecting my thoughts.

“So tell me, what the fuck were you thinking you would accomplish if you killed my child?” I asked.

“Fuck you Janeiro, you are nothing but a black piece of shit,” Mr. Jiménz said. I turned around with my chrome 9mm in my hand.

“What the fuck did you just say to me?" I asked as I pressed the gun to his head.

“I said fuck you, you black piece of shit,” he said as he spit in my face. I was taken aback; never in my 59 years had a motherfucker spit in my face. I completely lost it; I started hitting him with the butt of my gun

“Don't...WHAM…you…WHAM…WHAM…ever…WHAM…in your…WHAM…WHAM…WHAM…fucking life speak to me like that again…WHAM.” Next thing I knew, my son was holding me in a bear hug.

“Just let me go Stacey, I'm done; this motherfucker is lucky I don't kill his ass. Somebody get his ass up and throw him in the fucking dungeons. I don't want to see his ass because I promise I will end up killing him.”

*

"Stasi, what do you plan to do about this bullshit," I said as I rubbed my hand.

"Papa, he needs to die.

"No no, you know what? We need to kill all of his family while he watches. That would definitely knock him straight and teach him the Boudreaux's are not to be fucked with. Stacey, have his family flown here ASAP; tell them we are flying them on vacation so they all come," I told my son.

"I want to know what part of his crew knew the plan, because I'm going to kill those fucking bastards too for not saying anything. What if Stacey wasn't in the truck with me? I would be dead laying in a car stinking," my daughter told me.

CASEY

I'm not going to lie; I was really in my feelings about not knowing where Stasi was. I went by her office and her house, and she wasn't there. There was only one person that could get me out my feelings and probably give me a good meal too, and that was my grandma Alice. I decided to go ahead and go see my baby; I hadn't seen her in awhile. I U-turned at the next light and made my way to my grandmother's house. I pulled up to her house, hopped out, and walked right in.

"Grandma, what I told you about having your front door unlocked like this?"

"Boy shut up, don't nobody want my old tail, now hush and give me a kiss. I haven't seen you in a month of Sunday's, only way I know you're alive is when I look in my account on the first and the fifteenth and there's money in there."

“I know grandma, I will start coming around more, you’re the only person that I have in my life.”

“Are you hungry? I cooked some pork chops, cabbage, macaroni and cheese, and my homemade cornbread.”

“Heck yeah, I want a plate,” I said as I rubbed my hands. “I need to talk to you too,” I told her. I ran to the bathroom, not believing she was treating me like a kid. I washed my hands and went to sit at the dinner table.

*

“So tell me what you wanted to tell me, baby,” my grandma said.

“I just need your advice on something. I really like this girl; shoot, could probably say I already love her. I just want to be with her. We spent a few days together, and after that she has been so hard to get in touch with.” I started to eat, waiting for my grandma to say something.

“Well baby, if you like her, I mean really like her, what's stopping you from going after her? I know money isn't a issue with you, because you have it, so you should go to her. She can't do anything but tell you yes she wants to be with you, or no she doesn't, and that is plain and simple. But what I don't want you to do is get hurt, cause then grandma is going to have to kick your little friend’s fast tail,” she said while laughing.

“Grandma, you’re not kicking nobody's tail, you'd probably hit her with a spatula, but that's about it,” I said laughing.

“You’re right, you’re right, I would just hate to see my baby hurting, cause then I hurt. But if you want something you go after it, so after you eat that food, I want you out of here going to get your woman," she told me.

"I will grandma, I just want to savor this food, that's all, then I'm out of here heading for Haiti." I finished up and washed the dishes for my grandma "Alright grandma, dishes are clean. I love you and I will see you in a few days. You be safe baby, and when you come back by, bring that pretty girl with you so I can get some meat on her," my grandma joked.

"Will do grandma," I said as I kissed her cheek and headed for the door. "Oh yeah, I'm locking this door grandma stop, leaving it unlocked!" I yelled.

*

"Man, I hope she doesn't send my ass home," I said to myself. I drove to the airstrip so I could be on my way to Haiti ASAP. If this didn't prove I wanted to be with her, then I don't know what the hell would. I arrived and barely parked my truck before I was hopping out and heading for my jet. Lucky for me, I kept a packed suitcase aboard. I sat down and was ready to take off.

"Let's go, let's go! I got something to do," I yelled.

MARCUS

I can't believe that this man had really pulled a gun on me like did he not know who I was? I thought. I sat in Barnes & Noble reading this book called "*A Trap King's Wife by Jahquel J,*" and it was good reading, which was my way of calming myself down before I reacted without thinking. I had to come up with a plan to make sure Chris died for sure. I felt like he wasn't about to stop, especially after he got his daughter's head delivered to him. I needed to first find out who the fuck Carlee had texted, and whether or not they told someone the address. I closed my book and decided to text the number from the TEXT NOW app that allowed me to have any number I wanted.

ME: hey, I got a call from this number, I was trying to figure out who this was

904-213-0978: I didn't call anyone, maybe it was my little brother

ME: oh ok, it's fine, who is this though

RING RING…

"Hi, this is Susan, do I know you or something?" she asked.

"No, I don't think so, I thought this may have been my friend Carlee," I replied.

"OMG, you know Carlee? I know her too, she's in my class, she told me she was in trouble, so I told her dad for her.

"You told her dad what?" I questioned.

"That she was scared, and I gave the address she gave me," Susan said.

“Ok, well let me call her dad, thanks,” I hung up. Now that I knew Chris indeed had the address, I was just trying to figure out what he was going to do with it. I needed to find out where Javon was; I had to fill him in.

ME: Bossman, need to kick some knowledge (information) to you

Boss: At the club for the next 10 mins, then I'm headed to the crib

ME: Iight, I'll me you at the crib in twenty

Boss: 10/4

I knew he wasn't worried about Chris retaliating, but we had to make sure we looked out for the best interest of everyone that was invested within our organization. I hopped in my truck and headed towards Javon’s house, going over these thoughts in my head over and over. I still couldn't believe I killed a kid. I just hoped that I didn't have to kill anymore, because I don't know what the fuck I'd do. I wondered if Ms. Williams honestly didn't call anyone. I may have to have someone staying with us so when I'm gone she can be watched.

Me and Javon pulled up at the same time. I followed his car into the garage as he closed it, and we both stepped out our cars.

“What's up bruh, why you looking so serious?” he asked.

“I'm chilling for now, I just got a lot of shit on my mind,” I told him as we walked into the house. We sat down in the living room so I could tell him everything I discovered.

“Alright, so I found out that the mystery number belongs to Susan, one of Carlee’s classmates. Carlee texted her the address saying that she was scared something was going to happen, and to text her dad the address.

“Ok, so why didn't he come to the house then?” Javon asked me.

“Well, the good thing is Susan didn't do that until after we were long gone, so if he went, he went to a house that was sparkling clean and empty,” I told him.

“Well I guess that is a good thing that we moved pretty quickly up out of there,” Javon announced.

“The next thing I wanted to tell you, I'm not sure if you heard me at the shop because you were in your thoughts; but anyway, I'm riding down 103rd making my way to Cassatt. I pull into the gas station, and Chris' ass pulls up behind me talking a whole bunch of bull, then this boy pulls a damn gun on me telling me if I don't help him find his family, he's going to kill me.”

“That man ain't crazy, but we might have to move y’all and set up something so we can do a ransom call to let him know we got his people,” he told me.

“That sounds like a good idea bruh, because he thinks somebody is supposed to just find them while he does nothing; fuck that. But what's up, what's good with you–any news?”

“Yeah, so we got us a cop on the payroll,” Javon told me.

“Word, who? And how the hell did you manage that?”

“Detective Sands, and I didn't do nothing, he just waltzed in here the other day putting me on game about some shit. Matter of fact, I need you to get some killers together; we got to do something a little later that will help Casey and Stasi out big time."

"Iight, no doubt. Let me get on that now, what time we riding out?" I asked.

"As soon as the sun goes down; we got to be quick and precise, no fuck up's."

"Cool, I'll meet you here about 7:30l be easy, and if you need me, hit my line," I said. I gave him dap, and I was out.

STACEY (FORMERLY THE SPY)

Man, my pops was a beast. I guess you could say that was where I got it from. Jiménz had me fucked up if he thought shit was going to be cool; he was set on killing my sister.

"José, I need you to gather all of the Jiménz family; let them know that we are sending them on an all-expense paid trip. They don't need anything–no money, no nothing, we're paying. Tell them Mr. Jiménz and Ashley will join them once they arrive."

"Yes sir, I will get on it immediately, is there anything else I can do?" José asked.

"Yes, also make sure all the security cameras are working, and that we have all the security guards at their posts; no one is to make a move until told."

"Yes sir," José said as he hurried away.

"So Ashley, do you know the names of the people that were supposed to help your dad takeover?"

"It was ummm, th th the twins that usually are his security."

"Well where are they now, why aren't they here?"

"I'm not sure. He probably told them to come late, or he probably told them not to come," she said.

"Well, what I want you to do is get them here, and ASAP. No excuses, do we have an understanding?"

"Yes, we have an understanding, what do I need to tell them?"

"Tell them your dad hasn't come and you're getting worried."

"Ok, I can do that," she said.

"I want them on speakerphone so I can hear everything."

*

RING…RING…

"Hello, what's up Ash?" someone answered.

"Pedro, I don't know what's going on, my dad hasn't showed up for the meeting. Why aren't you guys here?"

"He told us to not come, but we will be there in twenty minutes, ok?" Pedro said.

"Ok great, I'll be here," she answered.

"Are you ok?" Pedro asked.

"Yes I'm fine, I just want to find my dad," she answered.

"Alright, we got your back, we'll be there shortly," Pedro hung up.

*

"Alright bet, now all we need to do is get ready for them when they arrive, and we'll be good."

"Ms. Boudreaux, this is very unexpected, but you have someone by the name of Casey here to see you," José announced.

"OMG, what the hell is he doing here? Tell him to come down, José."

"Yes ma'am, I will show him the way," José said as he walked away. Five minutes later, he returned with Casey.

"I'm sorry Stasi, I know you have a meeting going on, but I had to come talk to you. I really like you, and I really want to be with you; not hearing from you the last couple of days has driven me crazy," he said.

"Omg Casey, this is so out of the blue. I want to be with you too, but we have some serious issues at hand." We filled Casey in quickly, and he was visibly upset.

"Alright, they should be here any minute; everyone has to remain calm, we can't blow this."

LIEUTENANT DAVENPORT

I don't know what's going on but all of a sudden, Julian has been acting funny.

"Julian, you ok my man?" I asked.

"Yeah I'm ok, just not feeling too swell," he said.

"Ok, I thought you had something going on that you didn't want to tell me. Anyway, I have something to tell you that I think you would like to hear."

"What's that?" Julian asked as he grabbed the phone to record just in case it was something good.

"Well I hired a private investigator to follow Casey to get something on him to arrest him. Casey went to Haiti, and I had the private investigator follow him there," I said happily.

"You got to be kidding me, Derrick–you sent a private investigator out of the country to collect evidence that would not be admissible in court? We could lose our fucking jobs, are you not thinking, man!" Julian yelled.

"I am thinking. Once he gathers evidence, I will find a way to make it stick!" I yelled.

"How are you going to explain how you have Casey D'Haiti on a wire tap with NO WARRANT?" Julian yelled. He made a point, but I didn't want to let him know that; I couldn't let him know that.

"Look Julian, we are going to nail them motherfuckers, and it will be over. I will find a way to make it stick, I promise," I said as I grabbed his shoulder. "You're my partner, so are you with me?"

"I'm with you as much as I can, but that's because I'm your partner; just know I don't fucking agree, and when shit hits the fan, you're on your own. I'm not going to be here, I promise," Julian said as he walked out the door.

I swear, he was up to something, and I would figure it out. I would not lose my job, nor pension because he didn't want to get on board–he would die first. Hmmm, that just might be a good thing to do. I could make it look like he was killed on duty. The wheels in my head were seriously turning; if Julian didn't get with the program, he was going to regret it.

CHRIS

"Lauren, Lauren, where you at, ma?" I yelled as I stormed in her house. I walked through the house, and I couldn't find her. "Fuck Lauren, where are you, say something!" I yelled. I walked back towards her bedroom and heard sniffling coming from the closet. I pushed open the door, only to catch Lauren about to swallow a handful of pills.

"Yo, are you out of your fucking mind, Lauren? What is this shit?" I yelled.

"I don't want to live without my babies, Chris," she sobbed. "They're gone, they're gone, bring them back."

"What do you mean they're gone? Who told you that shit!" I yelled.

"I don't know, I just feel so empty, like they're gone. I just want my babies Chris, bring my babies home," she cried.

"I promise I'm going to bring them home, or I'll die trying; you will have them here, ok?"

"Ok Chris, I just want to sleep, can you stay with me?" she asked.

"I'm going to stay with you, but I came to get you. I need you to pack some things. I got to get you out of here, I can't let anything happen to you."

"Ok, give me about thirty minutes. I want to shower and get ready, don't leave me Chris," she begged.

"I'm not going anywhere, I'm just about to call Samantha; she's going to have to go with us, because if anything happens to me, I need to make sure both of you are ok to take care of our kids." I sat on Lauren's bed so I could go ahead and call Samantha, so she could be ready by the time we left.

RING…RING.

"What's up Chris, you found out anything?" Samantha answered.

"What's up Samantha, no I didn't find out anything, but I need for you to pack some clothes and whatever necessities that you need so that you can roll with me and Lauren. I need to keep y'all safe."

"Why we got to go with Lauren's ass? You think you going to get a threesome out of me, boy?"

"Samantha, chill out with all of that. I'm trying to protect the mothers of my children. If you don't want to come, then don't come. I don't have time for the bullshit," I yelled.

"Ok Chris, damn, I was joking, I'll be ready by the time you guys get here, bye."

*

"Are you ready Chris," Lauren asked. I looked up and there was Lauren, standing naked as the day she was born. I couldn't help but look twice.

"Lauren, what are you doing Lauren?" I asked.

"I want you to make love to me, daddy," she said.

"Shit I can't, we got to go baby, you don't want to do this," I said; although I wanted to fuck the shit out of her, I couldn't take advantage of her. I knew she wasn't in the right state of mind.

The next thing I knew, Lauren was giving me head. I don't know when she had unzipped my pants, but she was giving me the best head I've ever had. She sucked the head, then licked the shaft. I had to lay back, because I swear I was about to nut. She started pulling my pants down, and I couldn't even stop her. I wasn't about to end up with blue balls stopping her, so I lifted up so she could take my pants off. I watched her reach on her nightstand and grab some Listerine strips.

"Yo, what the hell you about to do with those, Lauren?" I asked.

"Just relax, Chris. It's not going to hurt, I promise." She put the strip in her mouth, and then started to suck my dick again. I swear, I didn't know whether to moan or cry; it felt so good.

"Mmmmmm," I moaned, "fuck girl," I said as I thrust my dick further in her mouth. I swear, once I did that, Lauren started to go wild; she took my whole dick in her mouth, and started playing with my balls, then she started sucking on my balls and that was it.

"I'm coming, Lauren!"

She stopped sucking for a second, and said, “Come for me, come in my mouth,” and with that, I nutted and she swallowed it all.

“I feel better after that,” she said as she walked in the bathroom to brush her teeth. She came back out with clothes on and her hair in a ponytail. “Help me pack Chris, so we can get out of here. I'm ready to relax, babe.”

“Alright ma,” I said as I got up and pulled up my pants. I was drained, but I couldn't let her know that. I helped her throw clothes and toiletries in her suitcases, and we got ready to head out the door.

*

“Chris, I just want to let you know that no matter what happens, I don't blame you for anything, and I know you've tried your hardest to always protect us, and I just want to say that I love you very much,” Lauren said as we walked to my car. As I put her suitcases in the trunk, I couldn't help but think about the what-ifs of what could've happened to my babies.

“I love you too Lauren, and I apologize that I didn't do better to protect you all, but I will give my last dying breath to make sure that you all are ok,” I told her honestly. I started the car as we headed towards Samantha’s house. “Let me apologize now for Samantha’s actions. I don't know how she's going to act because both of you are going to be in the same place together, and for some reason she hates our relationship with each other.

“She'll be ok. At this point, I could give a fuck about her, I'm worried about our three kids, that is all; she can stay in her feelings for all I care.”

We drove in silence the entire ride to Samantha's apartment. We pulled up, and I honked the horn for her to come out. While we were waiting, I went ahead and popped the trunk. Samantha came out with an attitude off bat; all I could do was shake my head–this was going to be something else. I just prayed she kept the drama to a minimum; I wasn't up for the extra bullshit. She threw her suitcase in the trunk and slammed the trunk.

"Aye, chill out with that bullshit, man. What's your problem already?" I yelled.

"Nothing Chris, let's just go; where are we going anyway?" Samantha asked.

"We're going to Savannah, Georgia. I found a nice house for rent out there. I already paid it up for the year, as well as utilities," I said as I pulled out of the parking lot.

"Good, at least we'll be away from here," Lauren said.

"You're right about that," I said as I headed towards I-95N. *This is going to be a long two and a half hours*, I thought to myself as I turned on Mytenacity radio to hear the Mid-Day mix.

MARISSA

I made it to Stasi's airstrip, but her pilot told me he took her and her brother to Haiti around six this morning.

"Brother?" I asked, "you sure it was her brother and not her security or something?" I asked.

"I'm pretty sure she said her brother, ma'am; maybe I could be wrong," he said.

"Ok, well thanks very much for letting me know, you have a wonderful day," I said as I walked away. I felt like I was a big shot with Javon's boys following me; I turned around and filled them in on my plans for today.

"Ok boys, I have an appointment that I need to be to, so I'm about to head over to San Jose to my doctor's office. If you don't mind sitting in an OB/GYN's office, then you two are fine to follow me inside; if not, you can stand outside. It is totally alright with me."

"We are following you everywhere you go, Mrs. Burns, unless it's the bathroom," one of them told me.

"Well first it's Ms. Gonzalez not Mrs. Burns and if you're going with me let's head to my appointment before I'm late," I said as I walked to my truck. It was going to take me a good twenty minutes to get to San Jose in lunch traffic all the way from the Cecil field. I half sped, half did the speed limit towards San Jose, making it just in time. I found a parking spot soon as I turned into the parking garage. I hopped out, hit my alarm, and made my way inside to go ahead and sign in so I wasn't waiting forever.

*

I was livid. I had made it to my appointment twenty minutes early, yet I had been sitting there for an hour and thirty minutes past my appointment time. I got up and walked up to the window to find out what was going on.

“Yes ma'am?” one of the nurses asked.

“I'm just trying to find out what is going on, my appointment was an hour and twenty minutes ago. I was here twenty minutes early as well, yet I'm still here” I said trying not to snap.

“I'm very sorry Ms. Gonzalez, we're a little short staffed; however, you are next,” she said.

“Well it would be nice if you let your patients know that. I could've left and gotten me lunch all the time I've been waiting. Next time, if I have over a thirty minute wait, or if you’re short staffed, please let me know as soon as I sign in,” I told her as I turned to walk to my seat. I let the guys know what was taking so long; they were pretty much nonchalant about it since they were just doing their job.

“Ms. Gonzalez, you can now come to the back,” the nurse called me.

“Ok guys, it's not a request it's an order; sit here and I will be back,” I told them. I walked towards the back so she could take my weight, my blood pressure, and give me a cup so I could take a urine test. I hated doing all of this; it seemed so unnecessary just to get my birth control pills.

“Alrighty Ms. Gonzalez, Can you give me a sample in this cup and place it in the window? When you’re done, you’re going to be in room three. Please get undressed from your waist down,” she told me as she walked away. I went in the restroom and gave a sample, placed it in the window, and washed my hands. I went to the room she told me would be mine, got undressed, and waited for my doctor to come in. No sooner than I sat down did my doctor walk in.

"Well hello Ms. Gonzalez, how are you?" he asked as he looked at my chart.

"I've been well, Dr. McCall, how have you been?" I asked.

I've been well, thank you for asking. Well, we have been trying to contact you for the last month; however, the number we have is disconnected. We needed to get you in for some additional blood work; your blood work from your last visit was looking a little funny when we ran it to check for HIV/AIDS. This is not to say that you have either, but in order to be sure, we need to run a test ASAP, which would be back within 24 to 48 hours. Is that ok?" he asked.

"Yes sir, that is definitely ok. I will go as soon as I leave here."

"Great, now like I said, it's not to say you have it by any means, so I don't want you to panic," he said.

"Yes sir, I completely understand; is it ok for me to get dressed so I can go down the street to Quest Diagnostics now?"

"Yes ma'am, I will have the paperwork you need at the window with the nurses," he said as he walked out.

*

I got dressed and walked to the window to get the necessary paperwork. Once I got the paperwork, I walked towards the guys and let them know it was time to go. As we headed out, we saw a red Nissan speed out of the parking lot. Both of the boys surrounded me before I could even say anything. They walked me to my truck, and checked the gas tank and the outside of the truck; I guess they didn't see anything that was out of the ordinary, because they told me it was ok to get in. I got in my truck and told them I would be heading back to the house. I attempted to start my truck, but it wouldn't crank I took my key out and put it back in again, this time hitting the gas. My truck finally started.

"Alright boys, follow me, I'm ready to go." I put my car in reverse, and the next thing I know…

BOOM

"Omg omg help help!" I couldn't get out of my seatbelt, and the front of the car was starting to catch on fire. I was going to die; I didn't have a chance to tell my best friend I love her. I was going to burn to death; Lord, this wasn't what I envisioned. My eyes were starting to burn, and I couldn't breathe. The next thing I remembered was hearing the boys trying to pull the door open while yelling for Javon to get there ASAP before everything went black.

STASI

To say that I was happy would be an understatement I couldn't believe that Casey came all the way here to tell me how he felt.

"Ms. Boudreaux, I noticed some unusual activity coming from the north end of the house. Someone came through a window that it looks like was broken," one of my security guards told me.

"Ok, well find whoever it is and bring them to me now," I said. I walked to the bathroom and decided to go ahead and change my clothes, because it looked like I was about to have some fun.

I wrapped my dreads up with a scarf so they were hidden. I took off my dress and put on a tank top, and then my bulletproof vest as well as another shirt, and then I finished it off with some 7 jeans and Timberlands. I didn't want them to think that I was scared or worried, so I made sure I looked every bit of unbothered. I came back out, and was surprised at the person my security had. He was a private investigator that I had seen a few times in the city. I was trying to figure out why the fuck he was here.

"Well, to what do I owe this surprise, sir?" I asked.

"I was sent here to follow him," he pointed towards Casey, "to get incriminating evidence so that Lieutenant Davenport could put him in jail," he said.

"So you risked YOUR life to follow him to another country to get evidence that would be inadmissible in court because you didn't have a warrant?" I asked.

"Yes, yes ma'am, he told me that he would find a way to make it stick."

"Well, how were you going to get that done if you just came in?" I asked.

"Well, I went to his jet and placed a bug on his seat so when he sat down, it would stick to his clothes and I would be hear everything, and so would Lieutenant Davenport," he said. Casey pulled his pants off to search for the bug; he found it and smashed it to pieces. I pulled out my .38.

"Well, I guess this is the end of your trip," I said before I sent a bullet through his head. "Get him the fuck out of here, I want his ass sent back to the States in a box ready for Lieutenant Davenport to open, with a note that says *kiss my ass,"* I told my security.

*

I was livid. I didn't know what to do, because we talked about murdering Pedro and his brother with Casey, and I couldn't have them come up missing just yet–not until Davenport was dead.

"Ok, so here's the plan. Ashley, you are going to meet the twins and let them know everything is good, and that your father said he didn't need their services. You are going to send them on their way and come back, or you will die with the rest of your family, is that understood?" I asked with my gun to her head.

"Yes ma'am, I completely understand," she said as she headed upstairs.

I decided to head to the dungeons with my brother Stacey and Casey to get Mr. Jiménz; his family was set to arrive within the next twenty minutes, and I wanted him to witness this with his own eyes. I looked in, and he was balled up in a corner; served his dumbass right. I walked inside the dungeon and was surprised when I got close to Mr. Jiménz. He jumped up and grabbed me, and held a shank to my head. I kept my composure, but on the inside I was boiling; how the fuck was his hands out of the handcuff, and how did he have a shank?" I said to myself.

"I want you motherfuckers to let me go when my family arrives, or this bitch dies!" he yelled.

"Mr. Jiménz, if you kill me, just know that you won't leave this house alive, nor will your family. I will make sure that they all die a horrible death from my grave," I said calmly. He gripped my neck tighter in a vice to shut me up.

My brother and Casey were pissed; they both had their guns trained on his head, but he kept ducking behind me after he spoke. I tried to think of how I could get him to let go without having him hurt. I wanted him to die a slow, agonizing death for this. I shook my head in a way to let them know not to shoot him. He was going to pay; I decided I would use a method I learned in defense class. I coughed, which made Mr. Jiménz loosen his grip, and then I went in for the kill. I slammed my foot down hard, which made him completely let go and bend over. I chopped him in his throat, and then slammed my elbow in his back; he was down on the ground within seconds.

My brother ran to get him up so we could head back to the table, but we started to hear gunfire coming from the meeting room. I screamed PAPA and ran towards the room; my brother shot Mr. Jiménz in his foot, took the shank, and handcuffed him to a pole in the dungeon before he locked the door back.

JANEIRO

I decided to call the few cops I had on my payroll at the Jacksonville Sheriff's Office to find out what was going on with this Lieutenant Davenport that was trying to frame Casey. I was so caught up in my conversation that I didn't hear anyone walk up behind me.

CLICK CLICK

"So Janeiro, we hear that our good friend Jiménz is in danger; where the fuck is he, and don't fucking lie to me," Pedro said. I hung up my call and attempted to turn around.

"No you don't motherfucker, don't turn around, just tell me where Jiménz is!" he yelled.

"Look, I don't know what you're talking about. Ashley called you guys for me because she said you were trying to kill me and my daughter and take over. Ashley set you up, my man." I could see him turn around from my peripheral vision, so I turned around and delivered a haymaker to dazzle him for a minute. He fell back holding his face, so I grabbed his gun and let off two shots

POW POW.

I shot Ashley right in the head, and Pedro's brother in the neck, so he was laying on the floor trying to put pressure on the wound. I didn't want to kill Ashley, but she was foul as fuck for doing what we told her not to do. I heard someone running towards the room, so I stood against the wall, not sure of who was running. My daughter ran in the room with Casey right behind her, and my son came right after.

"What the fuck happened?" Stasi asked.

“Ashley told Pedro and his brother that Jiménz was in trouble, and she brought them down here.” I pointed to Pedro. “He held a gun to my head; he lost sight for a moment, so I caught him off guard.”

“Well I'm glad you’re ok,” Stasi said as she hugged me. We were so caught up in talking that we didn't notice that Pedro had grabbed a gun from his ankle holster, and before we knew it, four shots rang out.

POW.POW.POW.POW

I heard Casey yell Stasi’s name, and I felt a sharp pain in my head before I felt myself falling, then everything went black.

JAVON

I was confused as to the call that I just got. I was trying to figure out why the fuck was I getting a call telling me that Marissa’s car just exploded, and she was being rushed to Baptist Downtown. Ain't no way my girl hurt and these two motherfuckers are alive and well. I was literally doing 100 to get to the hospital, and at this point I couldn't give a fuck if I was pulled over. I made it to the hospital within 10 minutes; I went to the ICU, and they put me waiting in the waiting room because she wasn't quite ready to have visitors. When I walked into the waiting room, the idiots of the hour were sitting there with their heads down.

“So please, explain to me why the fuck one of you idiots aren't laid up in a hospital along with my girl, I’m confused!” I yelled.

“Boss, we checked her truck, we didn't see anything and she wouldn't let us ride with her; she said she didn't feel right with a man in the passenger seat if it wasn't you,” he said.

"Well you should've called me, and I would've told her to let one of you ride; this shouldn't have happened, and if she doesn't make it, then you already know what happens," I said.

*

I had been sitting in the waiting room for over an hour, and no one had come out yet. The doctor finally came out saying her last name. I stood up, but he looked at me and said, "I expected her family. If you aren't her relative or husband, I will not be able to give you any information.

"Well can you just tell me if she's going to be ok?" I asked. He looked at me and told me he could not disclose that before he walked off. I was pissed; this was my girl, and I couldn't find out nothing. I flipped over the chairs and stormed off; it was the best thing to do before I started shooting motherfuckers in there.

The boys were following me, but I turned around and told them that I didn't want them leaving. I wanted their asses to stay with her until I got back; I had some shit to handle. I walked to elevator and waited for it to come to the floor so I could head to the parking garage. It finally came, and I hopped on and pushed the button to the first floor. I got off the elevator, and all the hairs on the back of my neck stood up. I brushed it off as me being paranoid about my girl. I headed towards the parking garage, trying to remember where the hell I parked my car. Once I got to my car, I noticed the light surrounding the area where my car was at was somehow busted all of a sudden. As soon as I opened the car door, I was punched in the back of my head.

"What the fuck!" I held my hand and attempted to grab my gun.

"I wouldn't do that if I were you," I heard someone say.

“Well beat my ass or shut the fuck up,” I said.

WHAM WHAM

I was hit in my stomach; it hurt so bad that I doubled over. I attempted to stand up, but a bag was placed over my head. I started swinging my hands to try to grip the bag, but I swear I was losing all the oxygen I had left, and all I could see was stars before my body went limp….

KAYLEN

I was starting to get worried. I hadn't heard anything from Javon, Stasi, or Marissa in the past three days. Stasi was supposed to be back from Haiti two days ago. I decided to turn on the news to see if it had anything interesting on there today.

"Thank you for tuning into the channel four news today; we going to update you on a car bomb that happened three days ago; we'll be back at 11.

Fuck! I couldn't wait until 11–that was an hour away. I had a bad feeling about this. I pulled up news4jax on my phone and searched for the car bombing, and low and behold, it was about Marissa. *Fuck! Fuck! How the fuck did this happen, man?* I threw on some shoes, not giving a fuck how I looked. I had to get to the hospital and be with my friend. I wondered if that was where Stasi was. I decided to just text her, just in case she was there and just didn't text me.

ME: hey I'm otw to the hospital, Marissa was in a car bombing, I don't know if you're there or not, but if you are I'll see you in a few, if not get here as fast as you can, love you and be safe, see ya soon.

I waited to see if I would see the three iMessage dots appear as if she was texting back, but it didn't show. I just decided to go ahead and head there. I got to the hospital quick; luckily, my condo was around the corner. I found out her room number, but they weren't allowing any visitors with her at the time. I went to the waiting room, and there were two of Javon's young bulls.

"Hey guys, where is Javon?" I asked.

"We don't know, we haven't seen him since he left here," one of them said. *What the fuck is going on here.* The doctor came out, and lucky for me, it was Javon's cousin-in-law.

"Hey Teedra, how's everything with you honey?" I asked as I gave her a hug.

"It's going good, are you the only one here for her?" she asked.

I guess so; I can't get in touch with anybody."

"Well it's not looking good; she may not make it. She has third-degree burns on her right side, and first-degree burns on her left side. We placed her in a medically induced coma, because she would be in a tremendous amount of pain," Teedra said.

I just didn't know what to do. I just wanted to find my friends. I couldn't help but cry; it was becoming all too much for me to handle. I got on the phone to start making calls. I was going to find my friends, even if it killed me.

CHRIS

We had been in Savannah for a good three days, and I thought it was about time for me to make a little noise in Jacksonville.

"Alright y'all, I've stayed low for a few days to make sure you both were comfortable, but I gotta go. I'll be back later tonight." Lauren and Samantha both told me to be safe and gave me a hug and kiss; I was glad they were getting along for the most part. I headed out the door and made my way back to Jacksonville; I was headed to fuck up Casey's world. I powered up my phone, and several text messages came through.

Melvin: Yo where you at C, we got that nigga Javon at the warehouse, what's going on, hit me back

*

Melvin: Yo we got Marissa, she died in the car bombing, now who don't know how to handle shit

*

Melvin: Package came for you and Lauren this Am

*

I decided to not even text; I'd talk to him once I got to the warehouse. Two hours later, I pulled into my destination. I was outside of Casey's grandmother's house. Since I knew where Javon was, it was about time to bring Casey out of hiding too. I sat and waited about forty-five minutes until his grandmother pulled up; lucky for me, she lived in a quiet neighborhood. I waited until she was at the door, and I bum rushed her.

"What in heavens name is going on?" she said as she dropped her groceries.

"Well hello, pretty lady," I said as I pushed her further into the house. I grabbed my gun and pointed it to her chest.

She just stared at me and said, "I don't have any money, so I'm not sure what you expect from me."

I looked at her and shot her twice in the chest before saying, "If you make it, tell your grandson Chris is looking for him." I walked out the house and got into my car; when I got two blocks away, I stopped at a payphone and called 911. If she made it, she made it; if not, oh well.

*

I pulled up to the warehouse, and everybody was there waiting like, they knew I was coming.

"What up what up," I asked; nobody said anything. "Nobody can speak, what the fuck is going on?" I snarled; my best friend and right hand came and grabbed me.

"It's important you see this," he said. He took me to two boxes that were stinking bad.

"Man, what the fuck is that? That shit stinks," I said as I covered my nose. Melvin just looked at me.

"Ok, I'll open it; somebody give me something to open it," I said. Someone brought me a box cutter; I opened up the first box and damn near passed out; it was my daughter Carlee's head.

"What the fuck!" I started crying, "You can't tell me this is my baby, no!" I dropped to my knees, but realized there was another box.

“Please don’t tell me this is one of my other kids.” I opened the box and almost passed out; it was my baby's arm. I couldn't believe this shit; my kid was five–she didn't do shit to anyone. “Why the fuck didn't you motherfuckers try to find me!” I yelled.

“We did’ everywhere you normally go, you weren't there. This was on the news for days; during the change of shift, they found her leg.” I was enraged. These motherfuckers were going to pay. I didn't give a fuck what I had to do; they had just sealed their death warrants.

To be continued......

TEXT UCP TO 22828 TO GET AN ALERT WHEN PART 2 DROPS!

CPSIA information can be obtained at www.ICGtesting.com
Printed in the USA
LVOW04s1641221015

459341LV00036B/1614/P

9 781517 422592